W9-CLM-108

RABBITSKIN

By Catturd

Thank you

enjoy

RABBITSKIN

Copyright © 2020 by Catturd, LLC

All rights reserved. No part of this book may be reproduced or transmitted in any form or by any means without written permission from the author.

ISBN 978-0-578-23117-4

Intro

As I look back on last June, it seems like a bad dream. However, since I'm wearing a straitjacket and locked in a padded cell, it must've been real.

My name is Logan Spencer.

A year ago, I was a corporate superstar, next in line to become President of Preotec, the largest corporation on Earth. We had the original patent on the Maze-O, which changed the world and single-handedly ended the age of the computer. In one day, computers became obsolete.

Harry Fox, the inventor of the Maze-O, quickly became the richest man the world had ever seen. He bought over half of what's left of Wall Street. Preotec currently has an unbreakable monopoly wrapped around the world's throat. That pisses me off.

It's only two months before the turn of the century. The year 2200 is finally here. Or is it? Unfortunately, I know something they don't know. This planet might not see the new century. You see, contrary to popular belief, I'm not crazy at all. I'm just the only one who's met Rabbitskin, and I know his secret.

In the morning, my captors will come for me and I'll be executed. They claim I'm a homicidal maniac who blew up corporate headquarters, killing hundreds and leveling a city block — well, I did blow it up.

Sometimes people with certain knowledge have to make desperate decisions. What I destroyed in that building might end up saving this sorry planet.

This dumbass shrink has been trying to dissect my brain all week. He thinks the months I spent lost in the wilderness somehow turned me into a Looney Tune. Boy, is he barking up the wrong tree. No matter how many drugs they pump into my veins, they'll never make me forget what really happened.

I know what you're thinking. I'm alone in a padded cell talking to myself, I must be insane. In fact, I'm not telling you this story — I'm thinking it.

3

Remember, I helped develop the Maze-O and currently have one secretly attached inside my brain. These mental midgets couldn't find it because it wasn't installed in its usual place, underneath the skin above the left temple. Everyone is going to hear my tale, one way or another.

After my execution in the morning, an alarm will sound inside every Maze-O around the globe. It'll be so loud that every twisted fuck who wants to see me die will instantly shit their pants.

This alarm is programmed to go off as soon as my heart stops beating. The second my lights go out, the story I'm now recording will be simultaneously broadcast across every Maze-O on the planet.

They only think they've silenced me. I'd love to see their faces when they find out my death has released the truth. I'd love to see them squirm.

I know I sound angry, but if they would've only listened, I could've warned everyone. My life may end in a snap, but the rest of you might not be so lucky. Your fate might take a path usually reserved for horror films and nightmares.

Chapter 1

Blow up one lousy building and suddenly no one believes anything you have to say. They only want to see you hung up by the neck.

Not long ago, people considered me a genius. Actually, I am a genius; I just don't look too smart wrapped in this ridiculous get-up they seem determined to keep me in. I hate white. I wore black when I was a corporate man. It made me feel more intimidating. Hell, it used to be my trademark.

I graduated valedictorian from Harvard, class of 2190. Most of my graduating class went to various Fortune 500 companies around the world to make their mark in the business world. Being only 16-years-old, and considered the smartest human on the planet, I could pretty much write my own ticket. Microsoft, A.R.M., Techno World and even the government was begging me to come on board. Join the team, they'd say, but I couldn't decide.

The day after graduation, I was packing my last bag when "he" walked in. He looked like a bum off the street, raggedy clothes, raggedy hair, bone thin, and unbathed. I thought he was the janitor and asked him to take out the trash.

"You're Logan Spencer," the stranger said.

Great, I thought. Now I'll have to talk about janitor shit, and I was late for an interview.

Before I had time to get rid of him, the vagrant spoke again.

"My name is Harry Fox," he stated. "Sorry about my appearance; I don't get out much. It's been a long time since I've been inside this dorm room. It still looks like it did 40 years ago."

Then it hit me. I realized who this trash man was — Scary Harry. He was somewhat of an urban legend around campus, the smartest person to ever roam the hallways.

Harry graduated as valedictorian back in 2150 at the ripe old age of 12. He refused to use a computer, never carried a book, and didn't take notes in class. Professors couldn't teach him much; they were more interested in learning from him. Even the most brilliant minds couldn't understand his theories. He was simply on a different planet. This scared them, hence the name — Scary Harry.

After he graduated, every CEO in the world was watering at the mouth. The money they offered him was staggering. The bidding war for the child prodigy was unprecedented. Unfortunately, while everyone was fighting over him, he disappeared, vanished without a trace. As far as I knew, this was the first time anyone had seen him since. I'll tell you one damn thing. It piqued my interest.

I pulled up a chair and nestled in.

"I'm listening," I told my uninvited guest.

"I know how you feel right now," Harry said. "Everyone's clawing at you, tugging, pulling, whispering little white lies in your ear. But this doesn't fool you, does it? Do you know why?"

I wish I could've given him an intelligent answer, show him how brilliant and articulate I was, but instead I hesitated, looked confused, and said, "no."

Harry sat down in the chair next to me.

"You're like I was years ago," he calmly explained. "Your ideas far surpass the people who seek you. They dwell in the present, you live in the future. This is something they'll never understand. Maybe I can offer you something a bit more up your alley. Give me a couple of days and come with me to my laboratory, and I'll show you what I've been working on for the past 40 years. It's going to change the world and finally kick-start the economy again. I could use your help."

Now he had my undivided attention.

They say that curiosity killed the cat. If that's true, I had a full-grown male tiger shoved up my ass. I had to know, had to see it for myself. What could this eccentric genius have up his sleeve? There was only one way to find out.

"How far away is this laboratory of yours?" I asked.

"It's only a couple of hours drive," Harry said, "but the plane ride will be a bit longer."

Plane ride? Where the hell was he taking me?

I didn't care much for flying. Many years ago, before the global financial collapse, people thought we'd be flying in rocket ships by now. Aircraft had come a long way, but they still hadn't invented one that made me feel safe. I took a deep breath.

"Alright I'm in." I said. "But I'm blowing off an interview with William Gates and he won't be happy. Besides being the richest human being alive, he's also a major dick. If I stand him up, they'll be no second chances."

Harry grasped me firmly on my shoulder.

"Logan, in a few months William Gates' shares won't be worth a nickel. You'll have to trust me. I've saved you from a huge mistake."

I stuffed an overnight bag with unwashed laundry and grabbed my laptop off the desk.

"Let's go." I said.

Outside there was an aged, outdated limousine with a massive fellow standing beside it.

"This is Ben," Harry said, patting the large man on his back. "He's my driver, cook, and pilot. He keeps everything on my island running smoothly so I can concentrate on my work."

Island? This homeless-looking dude owns an island? This was getting weirder by the minute. I hoped his place had running water. Maybe Harry didn't mind smelling like goat cheese, but I certainly did.

Ben opened the back door and we hopped in. My heart began to race. It made me feel alive. It made me feel good; damn good.

"To the airfield," Harry instructed, and with a loud, embarrassing pop from the old exhaust, we were off. My Harvard days were done.

On the way to the airfield, Harry bombarded me with unusual questions. I wondered how long he'd been secluded on his island; from the sound of it, a hell of a long time.

Ben never spoke a word. Unlike Harry, he wasn't much for gabbing. Every now and then I caught him suspiciously glancing back at me through the rearview mirror. Something told me he wasn't as dumb as he looked.

It wasn't long before we were at the airfield.

Now when Harry said air "field," he meant it. This was no airport. This wasn't even a good field. It was more like some poor farmer's backyard. Put it this way, I doubt it was on the official logbooks down at the F.A.A.

The shock from the sight of the deteriorated runway didn't last long. When I spotted the airplane, all my fears were instantly shoved in that general direction. Obviously, Harry's field of expertise wasn't avionics. Surely he didn't expect me to get on this V.W. with wings.

Surprisingly, Harry pulled a flask of whiskey from his shirt pocket and turned it up.

"Take a swig of this," he insisted. "It seems to help."

What the hell, I thought. I guzzled down a shot. It burned like a mother but helped calm the nerves.

Ben jumped into the cockpit and fired up the engine. I'd seen single prop planes in history books, but never thought I'd actually fly in one. I wondered if Harry had another pint of whiskey in one of his crusty pockets. I was going to need all the help I could get.

What made me get into that rust bucket is still a mystery to me. Under no other circumstance would I do this, but this was no ordinary circumstance. I knew in my heart that this was big. I couldn't quite put my finger on it, but I knew.

"Where's this island of yours?" I screamed as the engine roared.

"Don't worry," Harry yelled back. "It's small, but tropical. You'll love it."

After violently rumbling down the runway, we were soon flying. I have to admit, it wasn't that bad. The day was clear, and the coast was beautiful. We flew low and kept to the shoreline. The old engine purred, it's steady hum was nearly musical, almost hypnotic.

So many thoughts were running through my head. My imagination ran wild. My brain was bursting. What was Harry working on? What the hell could it be?

Many hours later, white sand and palm trees were in plain view.

"It won't be long now," Harry announced. "Less than an hour."

The son of a bitch had to know he was torturing me. I tried to play it cool.

That hour seemed like an eternity. Endless blue ocean flowed for miles. Water and more water passed beneath us until I was lulled into a half-conscious state.

Finally, Harry tapped me on the shoulder and pointed down.

"There!" he shouted. "There's my home."

The island appeared out of nowhere. It was magnificent. A white sandy beach surrounded the tiny land mass. A variety of tropical plants and palm trees were abundant and beautifully landscaped around a gorgeous mansion. I almost wet myself. I guess I expected to see a rickety tiki hut or something.

Ben circled the island a few times and went in for a landing. He pushed a red button which converted the landing gear to floats. Thankfully, the ancient relic had one modern feature. We landed smoothly on top of the water and gently eased up to a long wooden dock protruding from the beach. Ben jumped out and tightly secured the newly converted seaplane.

"Home sweet home," Harry said. "Welcome to Maze Island. Give Ben your bag and come with me to the house. We'll talk business first thing tomorrow morning. Tonight, we'll drink and dine. Ben's gonna cook up some of his famous smoked Spanish mackerel."

Although I was dying to find out what was going on, a night of rum runners and fresh fish sounded pretty good. I needed a night with no pressure and no interviews. Besides, I'd never met anybody smarter than me. Maybe someone could finally tell me something I didn't already know. I doubted it.

As we trudged up the sandy trail to the mansion, I couldn't believe how awesome this tropical hideaway really was. How could someone who dressed like a filthy street vendor, drive a beat-up antique car, and have the oldest plane on the planet live in a place like this? How could he afford it?

As we closed in on the mansion, the first thing that caught my eye was the swimming pool. It was straight out of the Garden of Eden. Lavish flowers littered the grounds and several waterfalls flowed through a massive pile of properly placed boulders. It was artwork. It was a postcard.

To make a long story short, inside the house was just as impressive, simply stunning. There was actually an elevator in the living room.

"Where does that go?" I rudely asked.

"That goes down to my lab," Harry said. "You wouldn't believe the money it cost to build simple things on an island."

Did he just say I wouldn't believe how much it cost? I'd believe anything at this point. Frankenstein could be downstairs, and I wouldn't even blink. I didn't give a rat's ass how much it cost. I only wanted to see its contents.

Ben led me to a bedroom and asked if I wanted to shower before dinner. I agreed, but I didn't want to bathe. Hell, Harry apparently never did, so why should I? Reluctantly I took one anyway, threw on some wrinkled clothes, and sat impatiently on the edge of the bed. This was driving me nuts.

Finally, Ben came and led me to the dining room. Harry was already sitting at the table sipping wine. I sat in the chair next to him and he poured me a glass.

"Okay," he said. "I know it's killing you. Ask me anything, but please allow me the pleasure of showing you my work in the morning. It's been a long day."

I didn't know where to start.

"How can you afford this place? Why did you disappear all those years ago? Why did you pick me? Who else knows about this place? How do you get your shower so shiny?" I wanted to know everything.

Harry slammed down his wine, let out a loud sigh, and began.

"When I was 12-years-old my parents were killed in a car crash," he sadly explained. "It's strange; when I look back now, I think it was all part of a bigger plan. My parents were billionaires and their wealth would one day fund my work. After the crash, it was all passed to me. I'd like to think what I've done with my inheritance would make them both proud. It hasn't been cheap. It's cost me almost every dime. Believe it or not, getting you here was about the last of it."

Great, I thought. I'm stuck on nutty island with professor fruit loop.

"As for who else knows about this place," Harry continued. "I'll assure you that besides Ben, you're the first to step foot inside my home since the builders left years ago. We do receive deliveries and supplies, but no one is allowed inside. Ben handles all maintenance and upkeep on the island. He's quite handy."

"But why me?" I asked.

"That's easy," Harry said, perking up. "I've been waiting a long time for someone like you to come along. Logan, I've been watching you for many years. Your resume is quite impressive. Your calculus formulas that shocked the world when you were only 8. The World Medal of Merit you received at age 10 for your work in physics."

Harry paused and looked me dead in the eyes.

"Tell me the truth, Logan; of all your great accomplishments, not one means a thing. Be honest, you've been holding back. You're afraid to try? I mean really try. You're scared of what you might dream up?"

Harry was right. I'd never been challenged. Every book I read bored me. There was no one alive who could begin to pick my brain. My ideas could never be mentioned to these brainless agitators who puked the same worthless theories over and over. That's why I couldn't work for any of those pushy companies. I was a thousand years ahead of them, and I didn't feel like babysitting the idiots. I didn't belong with them. Maybe this is where I belonged; with Harry.

Ben came into the room with two huge plates overflowing with his famous smoked delight. It was perfect timing. I was tired of thinking, tired of wondering.

During dinner, I hardly said a word. Ben was a hell of a chef. The Spanish mackerel was extremely fresh, no doubt caught from the island. The sauce ladled on top was heaven, and I soon forgot about everything except stuffing my face.

After dinner, Ben joined us by the pool for a nightcap. Work was never mentioned again that night. We knew it'd spoil the moment.

Soon I grew tired and excused myself. I went straight to my bedroom. The sooner I fell asleep, the sooner it would be morning, then I'd know.

Chapter 2

Dreams. I never understood them. Dreams are for those who have the luxury of letting their minds wander, an escape from reality. A true genius rarely sleeps, which eliminates the opportunity for the most part. You can bet I didn't dream that night on Maze island. Sleep wasn't an option. The thought of what was hiding down that elevator was tearing at my soul.

I realized what I had to do, what I must do; have a look-see.

I wasn't covert about it. I marched straight over to the elevator, got on, and pushed the down button.

When the elevator opened, I was staring at Harry Fox.

"What took you so long?" he said, pointing at his watch. "I'd almost given up on you."

I should've known. Great minds and all.

Harry led me down a narrow hallway to the door of his secret lab. I was so excited, I was about to jump out of my skin. I was now only seconds away from seeing what the child genius had been working on the past 40 years.

Harry slowly eased the door open, and there I was, standing in the midst of greatness — a half-empty room with a chalkboard in the corner. There wasn't even a computer in the damn place. This had to be some kind of sick joke. Suddenly, though, something caught my eye. There was something peculiar written on Harry's chalkboard. I strolled over to investigate.

Now, mathematics was my thing. There was simply no one better. I created mathematical theories the world had never seen, but I didn't recognize any of this.

"What the hell is that?" I asked.

"Foxtronics," Harry said. "I invented it. All my life people told me math was an exact science. I never believed it."

Harry grabbed a pointer and walked to the chalkboard.

"My formulas are centered around the number zero," he explained, pointing to an equation. "A number that's basically been overlooked for years. It's taken me places I never dreamed. It's how I invented Liquid Memory."

"Hold on," I said. "This won't be easy, but pretend I'm dumb for a minute. Let's start with Foxtronics, and go from there. I want to know everything."

Harry grabbed an eraser, wiped the chalkboard clean, and went to town. For hours he lectured me, and I learned. I was like a sponge, soaking it all in. I couldn't believe it. This weird dude was actually smarter than me — a hell of a lot smarter.

Zero; so much information stored in a number that represents essentially nothing. How could I have missed it? For the first time in my life I felt inadequate. Is this how normal people felt around me?

"Are you getting all this?" Harry asked during his presentation.

"Every last bit," I bragged.

"I knew you would."

I wanted to know more.

"What's Liquid Memory?" I desperately asked.

"We'll get to that after breakfast." Harry said, chuckling. "Let's go upstairs and have a bite. There's much to learn and we'll think better with some food in our bellies."

I didn't care about eating, but I didn't want to seem rude. I played along.

Ben had already prepared breakfast and was waiting for us upstairs. Harry spent most of the meal talking about an array of topics I didn't give a shit about. I only had two words burning inside my aching skull — Liquid Memory. I couldn't wait to get back downstairs.

Everything I thought I knew had just been turned upside down. With one stroke of his dusty eraser, Harry wiped clean every law of physics and math.

How could memory be stored into a liquid? I thought.

Harry took his sweet time, but finally finished his meal. I practically ran to the elevator. I was a mess.

Once back inside the lab, Harry picked up a tiny clear piece of film off a table. It looked like a flattened-out contact lens.

"Is that Liquid Memory?" I asked.

"No," he said. "This is a Maze-O, and it contains Liquid Memory."

I was stumped. This happened to me often around Harry.

I don't have to tell you what a Maze-O is. Today it's a household word. Practically everyone on the planet has one now. It's still hard to believe this is where it all started; in Harry's little laboratory on his prehistoric chalkboard.

Harry spent days showing me everything. He taught me about Liquid Memory, the Maze-O, Foxtronics, but more important, the Power of Zero. It was even hard for me to understand it all. For the first time, I had to really apply myself, push my mind into different places, stretch my imagination.

Two weeks flew by and we got little sleep. Harry was relentless, but I didn't care. I was high on learning, high on knowledge.

Every night after dinner we'd go outside, gaze at the stars, and listen to the ocean. Work was never discussed during this time. I grew fond of these hours. It was nice to take a breather after so much brain activity.

One night, during our break, Harry wandered over to where I was lounging.

"Tomorrow I'm going to attach a Maze-O to you," he said. "Then you'll understand. You're progressing faster than I ever imagined. I'm proud of you, son."

Without saying another word, Harry walked inside.

For hours I sat by the pool, wondering what it'd be like. It should work. All the numbers were there. Life on Earth was about to change. I felt small and insignificant. Honestly, I felt afraid.

I dozed off on the patio recliner.

I awoke at sunrise still on the pool deck. The morning was cool and the seagulls were screaming down on the beach. I leaped up. Today was the big day. I hurried to the lab.

When I arrived, Harry was sitting at his desk with my laptop nearby. He was holding an unusual device that should've belonged in a dentist's office.

"Let's get started," he said, kicking a chair in my direction.

I took a closer look at the object he held. I could clearly see the Maze-O thingy attached to the end. I leaned back in the chair and shut my eyes. I felt a sharp poke near my left temple. It wasn't too bad. I waited for some sort of impact.

There were no numbers flashing across my vision, no symbols nor sounds. I didn't feel any smarter, but I did feel something.

Harry turned on my computer.

"What's a subject you know nothing about?" he asked.

I thought for a moment.

"Cooking?"

It's true. I'd never cooked a meal in my life. If it weren't for pizza, I would've died years ago. Since my arrival on Maze Island, I'd been suffering serious pepperoni withdrawals.

Harry held the laptop where I couldn't see it and began logging in some secret information.

"Okay," he said. "Tell me all the ingredients for making Sautéed Chicken Cointreau."

"Yeah, right," I replied.

"Just do it," Harry insisted.

"Four cups of chicken broth. Two oranges, peeled, sliced, and seeded. Two ounces diced ginger. Four large whole chickens boned and skinned. One cup of mushrooms, sliced. Seven tablespoons butter. Half cup of Cointreau. Half cup of pea pods. Salt and freshly ground pepper."

Did I just say that? I thought. Where did that come from?

Harry smiled and turned the computer around. I was dead on.

"Now you know why Ben cooks so well," Harry said, grinning. "You want to try something else?"

"Ask me something crazy," I urged.

Harry got back on my laptop.

"How many games did Whitey Ford win for the Yankees in 1963?"

"Twenty-four," I answered. This was addictive.

Harry and I spent the better part of the morning confirming what I already knew. I had become a human computer. I was a walking, talking, souped-up Macintosh.

Technology was back!

Chapter 3

Anything that could be stored onto a computer, Harry could pour into his Liquid Memory. If information made a person smarter, the Maze-O could make anyone intelligent overnight.

With the snap of a finger one could know almost everything. It couldn't solve problems, however. Information still had to be dumped into the Liquid Memory before it could be accessed by the user. I was glad. I didn't want to become obsolete like computers were about to be.

That night Harry broke one of his own rules. He wanted to talk about work during our downtime.

He asked me one simple question — "Now what?"

"Think about what this will do to the world economy," Harry said. "Companies will go bankrupt. People will lose jobs. I've had years to think about this. Don't take this lightly."

"What do you want to do?" I asked.

"We could both use a break," he said. "Let's relax for a week and think about these things. Then we'll talk."

All day, I thought about what Harry said. He was right, you know. The Maze-O would make a lot of people happy, but it would piss a bunch of people off; important people, dangerous people.

The world had waited a long time for something monumental like this to happen. The 2030 global financial collapse had stopped nearly all technological advancements for 150 years. Stifled by the need to simply feed the planet, everything came to a screeching halt. Nothing had come along since with enough power to jump-start the global economy. That is, until now.

Talk about some good inside information. I can't lie; the thought of those goons down on Wall Street shitting their two-thousand-dollar suits gave me a stiffy. They were so sure of themselves. They thought they knew all the angles. Harry was about to throw them a curve ball Babe Ruth couldn't hit. Everyone had long forgotten about Harry Fox the child genius. That was all about to change.

During that week, many different scenarios played out in my mind. I thought about the Maze-O, the future, and my time at Harvard. I didn't care for school or the students. I never liked people much. Most were overrated assholes. I wouldn't be missed either. I had no family or friends to speak of.

I was abandoned at birth and dumped onto the doorsteps of a school for gifted children. I was raised by teachers, older students, and whoever else would put up with my shit. My inventive mind and sometimes bad attitude couldn't have been easy to deal with. I'm much easier to take in small doses. Although I never had a real family, like Harry, I never felt the need to be around people. I guess you don't miss what you've never known.

I loved Maze Island. Harry was wise to move somewhere so secluded. He would've never gotten the Maze-O off the ground in the cutthroat business world back on the mainland. If someone else funded his venture, they would've had a say-so. That would've been an instant death sentence.

This would only be the beginning of his problems. The FDA, EPA, lawyers, and other worthless agencies would've made his life a living hell, and in the end, they would all want a piece of the action. On his island, it was just Harry and his idea. There was no one to dilute his vision, no one to answer to. In short, there was no one to fuck it up. Harry must've seen this coming a long time ago. He was always 10 steps ahead of the game.

A week later, Harry and I met by the pool to discuss the future of the Maze-O. I had thought long and hard about our dilemma but wanted to hear his ideas first. You see, Harry liked asking questions he already knew the answers to. I had a feeling this was one of those times.

There was no wine that night. Supplies were getting low. It was crunch time.

As expected, Harry's plan was detailed, well thought out, and directly to the point.

Harry wanted to start with a surprise news conference.

"It's imperative to let the public know first," he stressed. "We damn sure don't want to present this to any government agencies or large corporations behind closed doors. Once those doors shut, they're impossible to open again. Regardless, we'll still have some serious problems. They'll be bureaucrats, religious nuts, and other habitual whiners coming out of the woodwork."

"How are we going to handle that?" I asked.

"Don't worry," Harry said. "The demand for this technology will be unstoppable. They won't be able keep it off the shelves."

For start-up money, to secure a fat loan, Harry would offer his island as collateral. He'd pay back the loan, in full, as soon as possible. Bankers always want control, but they wouldn't get it this time. They'd hate him for that.

All research would be done by Harry and I alone. We'd never discuss the Power of Zero to other scientists. Lesser men would try and copy Harry's lifework and use it for their evil purposes. This didn't worry me. In my opinion, besides us, no one would ever understand Foxtronics.

Harry's primary goal was to make this new technology available to everyone.

"Logan, the Maze-O's potential is endless," he told me. "But we must ease people into this. Basic information will be the first step. Anything we can dream up will be next."

Harry talked for hours, and when he was done, there was nothing left to add. He'd even set up a news conference for the following Saturday at noon. The wheels were in motion.

August 11, 2190. That was the day.

You remember. Everybody does.

I could talk about that day forever; the buzz in the air, the flashing of the cameras. The cat was out of the bag.

I stood beside Harry as he shocked the world. He looked bigger than life. He looked presidential. One after another the questions kept coming. He told them everything except how he did it. That was just Harry.

One reporter asked, "Where will this take us tomorrow?"

19

On that day we didn't care. Nobody did.

When the buzzards were finished with Harry, they started in on me. I wasn't as polished as him, but I held my own. When they asked me silly questions, I made them look stupid. Harry got a big kick out of this and continually snickered during my time at the podium.

The press conference dragged on for hours. By the time we'd finished, half the planet had tuned in. To this day, it's still the most viewed news event in history.

Whether we liked it or not, Harry Fox and Logan Spencer were now household names.

There was no turning back.

Chapter 4

Without my knowledge, Harry had been diligently working behind the scenes. While we were on the mainland, he'd sent Ben back to Maze Island to meet with a banker. With the island up as security, the loan was approved on the spot. Within days we'd get our start-up money.

After the press conference, Harry and I were picked up at our hotel and secretly shuttled across the state to the North Carolina coast. Harry had set up a private meeting with Scott Malone, one of the few people he'd kept in touch with all these years. He had a small manufacturing company that made computer components and anything else that paid the bills.

Mr. Malone's company was named Preotec, a family-owned business that had survived the global depression. It was built on the Malone guarantee, a firm handshake, and the unspoken law that the customer is always right. He had a whopping 20 employees. I thought the place was a dump, but kept my mouth shut.

Harry and Mr. Malone were happy to reunite and, after exchanging pleasantries, we were shuffled back to a cramped, dingy office. The musty room was bursting at the seams with family photos and cheesy plaques. One plaque actually read — *Genius At Work*. Oh, brother.

Mr. Malone was a likable enough fellow, one of those guys who always had the same unlit cigar stuck to the corner of his mouth. He was pleasantly plump and disheveled, but seemed comfortable in his own skin.

"Saw your press conference today," he mentioned, as we took a seat. "I didn't understand half of what you two brains were talking about, but if this Maze-O contraption can be manufactured, you've come to the right place. I can mass produce anything."

Maybe that was true, but the only thing I was sure Mr. Malone could mass produce was children. He seemed to have that down pat. I'd never seen so many pictures of crumb snatchers in my life.

Mr. Malone told us that he had 300 acres to build on if needed.

"Been in the family for generations," he bragged.

He slapped a weathered map down on his cluttered desk and showed us his plot. This kind of acreage was rare in this day and time. The old cuss was sitting on a gold mine.

The two lifelong friends talked for hours. Business was thrown in here and there, but they mainly spoke about the good old days. I'd never seen this side of Harry. I was glad we came to Preotec. This was good for him.

As the evening wound down and the war stories finally subsided, Mr. Malone offered us a room for the night. We gladly accepted. It was almost midnight when we arrived at his house, a cozy wooden structure with a huge wrap-around porch.

"Honey, look who I picked up on the side of the road," Mr. Malone shouted as we trampled through the front door. "Got any leftovers from supper? We've got some hungry bums to feed."

Mrs. Malone came out of the kitchen wearing a colorful apron. She looked like a corny cliché of a 1960s housewife I'd seen in movies.

"Harry, is that you?" she called out. "It's about time you came to visit us. I should whip your butt, young man."

The two hugged.

Mrs. Malone led us to the kitchen and began filling the table with homemade delights. I didn't want to be rude, but I just started digging in. I was tired of seafood. Unlike Ben's Liquid Memory meals, her cooking skills probably came from years of actual hard work.

After we ate, I was led to a small bedroom upstairs where I quickly passed out. It had been a long day, and I was exhausted.

In the morning I woke to the wonderful smell of bacon pouring through my bedroom. Unfortunately, when I pried my eyes open, there were two kids gawking down at me.

"What's your name?" a little girl asked.

"You want to see my new tractor?" a smaller boy said, sticking a tiny object two inches from my face.

I didn't know what to do. I wanted to scream for help. I'd never been around children before. I spent most my childhood alone solving problems.

"What's wrong, Mister?" the little girl said. "Cat got your tongue?"

Cat? I thought. What cat is she referring to? I didn't understand these tiny humanoids and their odd behavior.

Luckily, I was rescued by Mrs. Malone.

"You two get out of here and leave Mr. Spencer alone!"

The inquisitive duo ran away screaming their heads off.

"Come on down and meet the whole gang," Mrs. Malone said. "Breakfast is almost ready, young man."

To my horror, there were even more kids downstairs, lots of them. They were all persistent noise makers and dreadfully unsophisticated. I couldn't understand a damn word they were saying the entire time we were having breakfast. I was fluent in 20 languages, but couldn't follow their insane logic on any topic discussed. Mr. and Mrs. Malone, however, had no problem deciphering their strange dialogue, even when all 10 were speaking at once, which was most of the time.

In the middle of breakfast, there was a loud knock on the front door.

"I'll get it." I said. This was my chance to escape. I practically ran from the kitchen.

When I opened the door, I almost fainted. It was William Gates, the richest man on the planet. How did he find us?

"Now I know why you skipped our interview," Mr. Gates said, glaring at me with his cold, dead eyes.

Suddenly a stern voice rang out behind me.

"You're not here to see Logan," Harry yelled, stomping down the hallway. "You're here to see me."

"Is there somewhere we can talk in private, Harry?" Mr. Gates politely asked, changing his demeanor.

"Never was much for talking," Harry said. "I'm more of a hands-on guy myself. But thanks for coming anyway."

Harry stepped forward and slammed the door in Mr. Gates face. The thunderous boom sounded like a shotgun going off. I was so caught off guard, it made me jump back.

"Always wanted to do that," Harry confessed. "It's about time he got a taste of his own medicine."

Harry had just given the billionaire the shortest meeting of his life. It was over before it began. This was a noteworthy moment in history, the day William Gates was knocked off his throne.

You all know what happened next. Poor old Mr. Gates flew home in his private jet, drank a bottle of his favorite scotch, and blew his brains out with an antique pistol. Waste of a perfectly good bullet if you ask me.

For over 200 years his family had reigned supreme. I guess it was only fitting that his death would coincide with the end of the computer age. Microsoft and other companies like them were about to become extinct. Harry knew it, and evidently William Gates did, too.

His family fought over his money for years. Sorry bastard didn't even leave a will. Lawyers ended up with most of it. They always do.

It was time to say goodbye to the Malone family. If Mr. Gates could find us, the press would surely follow.

Ben was waiting for us at Harry's bank. The check had been cut. Time to get the Maze-O into production.

Harry's plan went off without a hitch. With Maze Island up as collateral, his eager bankers handed him a billion dollars without a second thought. They had their eyes on the prize and fully expected bigger and better deals in the future. Little did they know that soon Harry would pay them back in full, form his own bank, and become totally self-reliant.

Harry actually had the balls to call his bank — The Bank of Harry. This was hilarious to me, but no one else was laughing. Wall Street was getting nervous. Everyone wanted a piece of the pie, but nobody was even getting a bite. Instead, Harry was serving them all a shit sandwich, without the bread.

After the loan was secured, we flew back to Maze Island. Mr. Malone came along to inspect the product.

While we were on the island, as Harry predicted, a great moral debate was brewing on the mainland. All the news organizations were analyzing and re-analyzing. The religious freaks were predicting the end of the world. Some even said it was a hoax. Everyone had an opinion, but nobody could stop it. It was like a runaway freight train. People had to have it.

Harry made it clear at the press conference that he would make the Maze-O affordable for everyone. Mr. Malone told us that he could manufacture each unit for around hundred bucks; surprisingly low, but it was a simple object. Other than Liquid Memory, there wasn't much to it.

After many discussions, Harry Fox decided to sell the greatest invention of all time for a mere $500. He could've asked for $10,000, easily.

Harry allowed people to pre-order the Maze-O. The first week alone there were two billion requests. For those of you who didn't pass math, that's a trillion dollars. That's a shit load of greenbacks.

With that kind of money pouring in, Mr. Malone hired thousands of workers, and the first Preotec Mega-Complex was built virtually overnight. In the following years, hundreds would spring-up all over the globe.

The rest is history. Most of you know the story well.

Preotec flourished. Harry and I became filthy rich, and the Maze-O took over the world.

Chapter 5

No matter how many times I improved the Maze-O over the years, people wanted more. It was the planet's new drug. Before my sudden disappearance, I'd completed my best innovation to date — telepathy. People would now be able to communicate by their thoughts. As long as two people had Maze-Os, it would be possible, even from opposite ends of the globe.

Although Harry was impressed by my discovery, he didn't want this information leaked.

"It's gone too far," he warned. "We must draw the line somewhere. We must be responsible."

I think Harry was becoming afraid. He never dreamed I'd take his invention to such extremes.

Years back, Harry noticed I was getting obsessed with work and suggested we take a long vacation. That's how our annual trip to the Global Wilderness Sanctuary got started.

In 2057, the United States, along with Canada, set aside land so future generations could still experience nature firsthand. The great state of Alaska and the western regions of Canada were made into a huge nature preserve.

The government didn't run the current residents off their land; they simply didn't allow new citizens to move in. Newborns were only permitted to stay until their parents died. In less than a hundred years, the park was human-free.

The Global Wilderness Sanctuary was vast, untamed, and a wonderful place to escape. That was the problem. To keep it natural meant only a handful of visitors were allowed inside at a time. This put an extremely large price tag on park privileges. One-week free roaming in all quadrants was 10 million dollars per head.

Starting around eight years ago, Harry and I would spend the entire month of July camping and hiking in the park. It was 80 million a pop, but what the hell. That wasn't even a day's wage.

From the beginning, we both fell in love with the park. Every year we'd leave civilization behind and head for the mountains. We'd rent horses, load pack mules, and wander around the great outdoors.

Like clockwork, every summer, Harry and I could be found deep inside the forest. It was like our birthday and Christmas all wrapped up into one.

As time passed, we became more and more eager for July to roll around, especially Harry. He'd become bored with his invention and spent most of his time in solitude. I was solely responsible for every advancement of the Maze-O after the first few years of production. Harry was merely the face of the business. I was the brains.

Harry slowly withdrew from people like he'd done almost 50 years earlier. The only exception was spending time with me on our annual camping trip. He would smell every flower, study every animal, and marvel at everything nature had to offer. Harry always had this freaky thing about the natural world. He just seemed to appreciate it more than everybody else.

Over the years, I became a superb woodsman, but Harry took it a step further. He purchased land near the park, built a log cabin, and went overboard buying horses, pigs, goats, and other farm animals.

He called his little spread the Getaway Ranch.

From the day it was built, Harry spent nearly all his time at the ranch. I didn't know it at the time, but he was spending months inside the Global Wilderness Sanctuary. He'd saddle his favorite horse Honey and disappear into the woods. He even grew a long, scruffy beard and began carrying rifles, knives, and other redneck gadgets.

I was so busy working I didn't pay much attention to him. Besides our summer vacation, I rarely saw Harry in the later years. In short, he didn't fuck with me, and I didn't fuck with him. I considered this to be a perfect business partnership. We were both content.

Do you want to hear something really funny? At our last business convention in Vegas, Harry came dressed in animal skins. I thought it was hysterical. Others, however, didn't share my sense of humor. His appearance, eccentricities, and lack of interest in Preotec began to make people worry. Harry didn't care. He eventually donated his island to a non-profit organization where it was turned into a museum. Tourists could now visit Maze Island to see where it all began.

Harry moved to his ranch permanently, and seemed to be content, until a year ago. That was the day everything changed.

I still remember that day as clear as a bell. Harry had sent word for me to come to the Getaway Ranch ASAP, said it was a matter of life or death. I dropped everything. This was out of character for him, and I knew something had to be terribly wrong. I sent for the corporate jet and anxiously flew across the country.

After the plane ride, I rushed to his cabin and slammed through the front door. Harry was sitting with his back to me looking at the fireplace. He didn't even turn around.

"What's wrong, Harry?" I shouted.

"Bigfoot." He grunted. "I saw him."

I remember thinking, Harry has finally flipped his lid; his mountain man act had gone too far.

I walked over to the refrigerator, pulled out a couple of beers and sat in a chair next to my friend.

"What do you know about Bigfoot?" Harry mumbled, staring blankly into the fire.

"About what the average person would," I said. "He's big, hairy, and smells like shit."

"Take a minute and scan your Maze-O before I continue. I've already done this, and you should, too.

To play along, I closed my eyes and began to learn the history of the legendary creature.

Bigfoot was a large apelike creature reportedly sighted hundreds of times in the United States and Canada, most often in the Pacific Northwest. Most scientists discounted the existence of Bigfoot and some supposed footprints of the animal were known to be hoaxes, such as those produced by Ray L. Wallace.

For more than 600 years people have reported seeing the hair-covered animal. Alleged footprints of the beast have been found all over the world.

Bigfoot is described in reports as 8-feet-tall, weighing 500 pounds, and covered in thick, dark reddish hair. Witnesses have described large eyes, a pronounced brow ridge, and a low-set forehead.

The creature is commonly reported to have a strong, unpleasant smell by those who claim to have encountered it.

Sasquatch is the Native American word for the creature. The Bigfoot figure is common to the folklore of the Northwest Native American tribes. They normally describe the creature as uncivilized, usually living in the woods and often foraging at night.

Native American Bigfoot creatures are said to be unable to speak human languages, using loud whistles, grunts, and gestures to communicate with each other.

In the Bigfoot myths of some tribes, Sasquatch and his relatives are shy and benign. They may take things that don't belong to them, but they don't harm people and may even come to their aid. Sometimes Bigfoot is considered a close guardian to these tribes.

Bigfoot legends from other tribes, however, describe them as malevolent creatures who attack humans, play dangerous tricks on them, or steal their children; they may even eat people.

Most native tribes feel that Bigfoot is part of nature and therefore should be left alone. They are extremely tightlipped about the subject, only passing knowledge and experience to future generations within their tribe.

Many still believe in the primate and think it's evolved alongside humans, becoming astonishingly adept at avoiding human contact through a process of natural selection.

To others, these facts point to a cultural phenomenon kept alive through a combination of the misidentification of known animals, wishful thinking, and the deliberate fabrication of evidence.

"Pretty much what I expected," I said when I was done.

"Did it mention that the creature can talk?" Harry asked.

"Don't be ridiculous." I said.

"I'm not being ridiculous," he insisted. "I'm dead serious."

Harry got up from his chair, walked to the window, and leered into the woods. He began to speak, never taking his eyes off the forest.

"I'd been deep inside the park for a couple of weeks," he recalled. "It was business as usual. I'd ride Honey during the day, build a campfire at dusk, cook up some grub, and bed down for the night. I was almost home when it happened, only 10 miles from here. It was getting late, so I decided to camp for one more night."

Harry stopped and looked at me.

"He's out there right now, you know, watching us."

"Who's watching us?" I said.

"Haven't you been listening?" he replied. "Bigfoot."

"How do you know?"

"Because he said he was," Harry mumbled. "Even mentioned us both by name."

Harry continued without skipping a beat.

"As soon as I made camp, a creepy feeling came over me, even Honey felt it. I was reluctant to stray too far for firewood but scraped up enough to get a decent fire going.

The rest happened fast.

From out of nowhere, a large, hairy creature walked out of the woods and started talking to me."

"Talking? Are you sure?" I interrupted.

"Yes, I'm sure." Harry said, getting flustered.

"What did he say?"

"He said, I've been watching you, Harry Fox. You and young Mr. Spencer have been busy little bees. Get Logan to come to your cabin tomorrow night. I'll knock on your door at 8 o'clock sharp. It's time we were all introduced."

Harry waited for a response. There was none. He had rendered me speechless.

"You better say something soon," he told me.

"Why's that?" I said.

"Because it's 8 o'clock."

Chapter 6

Harry had barely gotten the words out of his mouth when there were a series of thunderous knocks on the front door. The steady pounding sent shock waves through the rickety cabin causing the dishes in the kitchen to rattle and clank together. The stiff, wooden door creaked and moaned as the unrelenting thumps came one after another

I froze. I dare not move. I dare not draw a breath.

All at once, the knocking stopped.

"Well," a deep voice called from outside the door. "Are you two fine gentlemen gonna let me in or not?"

Harry causally strolled over, opened the cabin door, and in walked Bigfoot.

I tried to speak, but the only word I could muster was a high pitched, broken, "B Bigfoot?"

"I'm not Bigfoot," the creature insisted, brushing some dead leaves from his shoulder. "My name is Rabbitskin. I don't approve of that dopey name. It's improper and vile. Makes me sound so unrefined. The nerve of some bloody people."

I just stood there with my mouth open.

"You must be Harry Fox?" the apeman said, sticking out his hairy hand.

Harry shook hands with the beast.

"And you must be young Mr. Spencer. Glad to meet you, good sir."

Rabbitskin marched across the room and plopped his butt down on the kitchen table.

"Harry, would you be good enough to put on some hot tea, sir. I've been stomping around the woods all day and would love a cup. This walking around barefoot is for the bloody birds."

Harry ambled to the kitchen and tossed a teapot onto the stove. While waiting for the water to boil, he nonchalantly handed us cups and saucers. Harry didn't seem fazed by any of this. Was he in shock or what?

Either way, I was apparently about to have a tea party with the smartest man alive and an overly polite Yeti with an English accent.

After uncomfortably sipping on some tea, I finally got up the nerve to speak.

"Rabbitskin. I've got a question."

"What is it, fine lad?"

"Who the hell are you and what the hell is going on?"

"That's what I thought you'd ask." Rabbitskin said, snickering. "But with less curse words, I would hope. You're much too intelligent to be talking like a peasant, Mr. Spencer. Please mind your manners, sir."

The situation had just gotten worse. I was now getting scolded by a stuck-up ape.

Rabbitskin slammed down the rest of his tea, and gently placed the cup and saucer onto the table.

"It's simple," he said. "I'm a scientist like yourself."

"A scientist? From where?"

"Rabistca," Rabbitskin replied. "I'm a representative of our planet's scientific community. The Maze-O was Harry's invention. Humans were ours. I was sent here 600 years ago to observe. Remarkable how far humans have come on my watch. For millions of years we've tried many species on your planet. Dinosaurs were a complete and utter failure. Ghastly creatures. What were my ancestors thinking back then?"

"Wait a second," I said. "Slow down for a minute. You said you invented us? What does that mean?"

"Although our appearance is primitive to your eyes, our technology far exceeds anything you can imagine. Years ago, humans were grown in our Green House laboratories. Incubated and tested. You're the most interesting life-forms we've ever created, but also the most destructive and cruel. That's why we only allow you gents to roam on one planet. Sorry to say, you're too unpredictable."

It was hard for me to absorb what I was being told. If Rabbitskin was telling the truth, though, everybody had been wrong about our creation since the beginning of time. Scientists, archeologists, and every religion were way off base.

I hadn't felt a rush like this since I was shown the Maze-O. From the look on Harry's face, this was his first; the first time he wasn't the smartest person in the room. I was starting to enjoy this.

"You've got our attention," Harry said. "But why have you revealed yourself to us? Why now?"

"That's easy," the apeman replied. "It's the Maze-O, good sir."

"What's that got to do with anything?" I muttered.

"It has everything to do with our meeting, young Mr. Spencer. Humans have come up with some interesting inventions over the past few centuries. For years, we thought you'd never evolve. Of course, we can't help you in any way. It's our most strict policy never to interfere with species we colonize on other planets."

"Did you say planets?" I asked.

"We've colonized thousands of planets with many different species throughout our history," the apeman explained. "Like you, scientists of Rabistca are dedicated to their chosen fields of study. I'm no different than someone on your planet who studies spiders or plants. I'm a Humanologist. I only study humans. You're my specialty. Like I said, I've been here watching your race for 600 years."

"How's that possible?" I grunted.

"Our average life expectancy is around 1,200 years or so. I'm 937-years-old. Our longevity is a mystery to us. We've been successful at growing species that live 300 years, but despite our faithful efforts, everything grows old eventually. Father Time's tough to beat. Even for us."

"What about life that occurs naturally on other planets?" Harry curiously asked. "Do you study them, as well?"

"I hate to tell you gentlemen this," the apeman revealed. "But there are no other life-forms in the galaxy other than the ones we create."

"How do you know?" Harry questioned.

"We've been roaming the universe for millions of years. We've never found that life merely happens. Believe me, we've tried to find natural life but there's simply nowhere else to look. Besides my species, natural life doesn't exist. In other words, my race didn't create the universe; just every living thing in it. Animal, plant or human. If we didn't grow it in our labs, it doesn't exist. Period."

"Harry," I said. "Do you have any whiskey?"

"Make that three," Rabbitskin agreed. "You humans do make some fine whiskey. I'm kind of partial to Jack Daniels myself."

Harry fetched a bottle and we began passing it around. Can't say that drinking after Sasquatch didn't gross me out a little, but the fact I was already numb probably helped. Not a single word was spoken until the pint was completely gone. Of course, Rabbitskin took much bigger swigs. He wasn't kidding about liking his whiskey.

After we were finished, Harry walked over to Rabbitskin.

"Mr. Rabbitskin, do you mind if my colleague and I walk outside and talk for a minute? This is a lot to take in. Please allow me to consult with my partner, in private. This means no disrespect to you."

"Why of course, sir." Rabbitskin said. "Take all the time you need."

Harry and I tiptoed outside and shut the door behind us. My first instinct was to run like hell, but I knew it wouldn't do any good.

"Are you okay?" Harry whispered.

"I guess so." I whispered back. "Do you think this could be true, Harry?"

"What does your gut tell you?"

"I believe it," I said. "Every last word."

Harry stood silent, rubbing his fingers across his scruffy whiskers. When he finally looked up, his whole demeanor changed.

"Logan," he said, in an official tone. "Things are about to get a little crazy, especially for you. But we're still scientists. In the last few hours you've gained more knowledge than anyone before you. You must take this opportunity and run with it. The business doesn't matter anymore. You must pay close attention to all this."

Now, I was really confused. This was no time for Harry to be talking in riddles. I didn't have time for this right now. This meeting was adjourned.

We walked back inside to find Rabbitskin in the kitchen rumbling through the refrigerator.

"Hope you don't mind, Sir Harry," the apeman said as he poked around. "I'm famished. Do you happen to have any chicken? My cousin's great, great, great, great grandfather invented them years ago. They've flourished on hundreds of planets. Good breeders. And by the way, the chicken did come before the egg. Thought you might want to know."

After our hungry houseguest had gobbled down almost everything in the refrigerator, it was back to business.

Harry was the first to break the ice.

"We understand who you are," Harry told the beast. "But why reveal yourself to us now? And what does this have to do with the Maze-O?"

That's easy," Rabbitskin said. "Since my ancestors have been testing life-forms, none have ever developed anything close to the technology we possess. You're the first. Frankly, we don't know how you did it. You two have created quite a buzz on Rabistca. Together, you've accomplished something unprecedented."

Rabbitskin pointed at me.

"Young Mr. Spencer has been busy for the past few years. He's taken your invention and ran with it, Harry. His latest improvement will allow people to communicate with their thoughts. This is an untapped technology we've never dreamed of having. Your invention could help my people tremendously. Although we've long perfected space travel, communicating light years away has always proved difficult with many time-consuming delays. We feel that if you two could work side by side with our top research teams, together we could take the Maze-O to new heights. Soon, our two races could communicate instantaneously by thoughts, with no delays, even from opposite ends of the universe. And that would only be the beginning."

I looked at Harry. He had a sly grin on his face. Maybe this is what he'd been waiting for all these years, someone to brainstorm with; someone to challenge him. I'd always had Harry to learn from. He had nobody. This is why he lived on a secluded island for 40 years and was now a recluse in the forest. It really was lonely at the top.

"How long will it take your research team to travel here?" I asked.

"Oh, they're not coming here, sir," Rabbitskin said. "We're going to Rabistca."

Chapter 7

Let's see? Travel to faraway, mysterious planet. Work side by side with a research team who created all living things. Yeah, I'm in.

I should've been scared, but I wasn't. The entire universe had just opened up to me. Harry remained mostly silent. He was probably calculating all this new information inside his oversized brain.

I was proud of my work on the Maze-O, but make no mistake about it, this was all about Harry. What I'd accomplished in the past few years, he could've done in a week. We were about to see just how smart Harry Fox was. To me, this was as compelling as traveling to another planet.

Think about it. Harry had figured out formulas that our Creators couldn't even come up with. Could Harry Fox be smarter than them? More intelligent than his maker? This was more complicated than Foxtronics or the Power of Zero. This was about Harry himself.

Anyway, that day, I thought I had it all figured out — Rabbitskin's ancestors were an ancient race of scientists. They needed to know why one of their experiments somehow jumped a million years ahead in evolution. I don't blame them. In the name of science, I would've done the same thing.

There was no need to tell Harry this. He was always a step ahead of everyone, even Rabbitskin.

Harry pulled up a chair next to our house guest.

"I'll help you," he told Rabbitskin. "But I want something in return."

"What's that?" the puzzled apeman asked.

"Knowledge." Harry stated.

"Knowledge? What sort of knowledge, good sir?"

"One thing in specific," Harry said. "How to grow and incubate life-forms. You see, Foxtronics is only the beginning of what I could teach your race. The Maze-O is only the first step. I have formulas that can unlock secret dimensions and take you to alternate universes."

Harry had dropped a bomb, but it was a firecracker compared to what was coming.

"It's true that Carnavorines such as yourselves created all living things in the universe," Harry told the apeman. "Your race has done well. But you didn't create the universe itself. Even you admit that."

Now, Rabbitskin was rattled. How did Harry know that his race of people was referred to as Carnavorines? He'd never told him that.

The apeman looked at me, searching for answers.

"Still don't understand who you're dealing with?" I said. "They call him Scary Harry for a reason."

Rabbitskin turned to Harry. "Nobody knows who created the planets, suns and moons, sir."

"I do," Harry said.

"Who?" Rabbitskin and I blurted out at the same time.

"Me."

Chapter 8

"There's only four of us," Harry revealed. "Our race is known as Godlings, but we call ourselves The Four. We come from a planet in another universe named Lorivox. Like the Carnavorines, our origin is a mystery to us. We've simply always been here. For billions of years we searched for answers. Where did we come from? Are we alone in the universe? Why were we even here? We seemed to have eternal life, but why? We became obsessed with finding out."

Harry told us that the Godling's quest to find life was basically all-consuming. To try and solve this puzzle, they began studying science, math and geography. After billions of years, they became smart; real smart.

The Four built great flying machines and searched every corner of their universe, looking for other life-forms. They found none. When there was nowhere else to look, they knew they had to try a different approach.

That's when Harry had a brilliant idea; why not try and find an alternate universe. Maybe they could find life there. The Godlings tried everything to make this happen, but failed time and again. They never gave up. Their loneliness drove them, and for countless years, they were relentless in their quest. That's when the number zero came to Harry. It was the answer to everything. That was the day he actually discovered Foxtronics. That's how he finally did it.

Harry never learned how to find alternate universes, but through the Power of Zero, he stumbled upon something better — how to create his own universes.

My head was starting to hurt.

I'd just gotten used to Rabbitskin's race being on top of the food chain; now this? I'd always said Harry was from another planet. I guess that was an understatement.

As the events unfolded that day, I became more and more excited. Rabbitskin, however, wasn't taking the news so well. This was his day to shine, and Harry had stolen his thunder.

I should've seen this coming. How could anybody from our planet be smarter than I? That should've been my first clue right there. This was getting good.

"Please tell us more, Harry," I begged.

"Please continue, sir," Rabbitskin agreed.

"I created thousands of universes." Harry told us. "But life wouldn't form in any of them. We were still alone. Alone in an endless void of planets, stars, and moons. Floating empty worlds filled with rocks and more rocks. Our very existence was bland and we had accomplished nothing."

Harry smiled at Rabbitskin.

"Then something unexpected happened. From out of nowhere, the Carnavorines were discovered in one of our manufactured universes. A universe we'd created millions of years earlier. We were overjoyed but had no idea where these unusual beasts came from. Strange hairy creatures with abnormally high I.Q.'s. We decided not to make our presence known."

"How long have you been watching the Carnavorines?" Rabbitskin asked.

"Forever," Harry said. "We began to monitor all the universes we'd created, hoping that a miracle would happen. Thankfully, it did. From the beginning, your people were fast learners. The Carnavorines never learned how to create solar systems, but the apemen could do something more special; create life."

The Carnavorines had been watching humans, observing without interfering. Little did they know, while they were spying on humans, they were also being watched.

I was beginning to feel small. Where did I fit in? Why was I even here? Harry could've obviously done this without me. I was no God like him, and to Rabbitskin, I was nothing more than a hamster on a treadmill. I deserved an answer.

"Where's the real Harry Fox?" I cautiously asked.

"Dead." Harry said, frowning. "I'm sorry, Logan, but he died with his parents in that car crash after graduating Harvard. Little Harry was thrown from the vehicle into a nearby lake and his body was never found. No one knew he was with his parents that day. People just assumed he was grief-stricken and disappeared to sort things out. He was soon forgotten. Sadly, humans have short attention spans."

"If you're not Harry Fox, what name would you prefer, good sir?" Rabbitskin asked.

"The Four have no names, but I kind of like Harry. It's starting to grow on me. Yes, Harry Fox will be fine."

Something wasn't adding up to me. Scott Malone and his wife had known Harry's father, even went to school with him. How could he fool these people? It didn't seem possible. They'd know the difference unless —

"I know who The Four are," I said out loud.

"How could you possibly know that?" Rabbitskin scoffed.

"Go ahead, Logan," Harry said. "Tell him."

"The only three people who could corroborate your story and make the whole thing sound authentic. The Four are Harry, Ben, Mr. and Mrs. Malone."

"Bravo." Harry said, lightly clapping his hands. "Good."

Harry got up, strolled to the front door and lightly tapped on it four times. The door immediately opened and in walked the other three members of The Four. They causally walked over, sat down at the table and didn't say a word.

Harry continued his story like nothing happened.

He told us that the Godlings had been on Earth since the early dawn of man posing as many different people and watching the Carnavorines. They were amazed at what the Carnavorines could do and finally felt fulfilled in this new world so full of life.

The Four were mostly surprised, though, that humans looked exactly like themselves. They weren't in disguise. The Godlings couldn't change forms. They couldn't explain this, so they patiently waited and watched humans slowly evolve. They also kept an eye on the Carnavorines. Rabbitskin's people, however, kept their formulas and affairs top secret.

The Four tried everything to recreate the Carnavorines' magic. They could easily make worlds, but this was totally different, apples and oranges.

Harry said that Maze Island had been their home for over a thousand years. It kept them away from prying eyes and allowed them to try and duplicate the Carnavorines' work.

"We never came close," Harry told Rabbitskin. "We still don't know how you do it."

The Godlings realized it was time they were introduced to the Carnavorines, therefore, Harry spent a year developing the Maze-O. Through the Power of Zero, he invented Liquid Memory; not for mankind, but as bait for the Carnavorines, a scientific way to be introduced.

I couldn't take it anymore. I needed to know something. Now!

"What the hell does this have to do with me?" I cried out.

Harry stopped in mid-sentence and looked over at me.

"You're number five."

Beads of sweat began to form on my forehead and my mouth became dry. I didn't like where this was leading.

"Okay, Harry." I said. "Spill the beans. What are you hiding? What the hell's going on?"

"As scientists, we marveled at what the Carnavorines had done with all living things." Harry told me. "They produced wonderful species, but they weren't greedy. They placed into every living thing the need to reproduce. A male and female were made for each species. Afterwards, they'd simply let them flourish as they may. Live and let live. This was of great interest to us."

"That's true," Rabbitskin said. "Once they're created, we never interfere with our creations, young Mr. Spencer."

"We never felt the need to reproduce." Harry explained. "Since we weren't grown in the Carnavorines' laboratories, this wasn't instilled into us. But we were intrigued. We studied humans' reproductive techniques for years. The Four was made up of three males and one female. It was decided that since I was the smartest, it would be me

42

and the female you call Mrs. Malone to try and produce a child. It's you Logan. You're my son."

Chapter 9

From the moment those words left Harry's mouth, my life flashed before my eyes. Suddenly, everything I didn't understand about my childhood became crystal clear.

I "was" dumped at a school for gifted children when I was born and never knew my parents. Could this be the reason? Could I be the son of a God? Harry's son?

Harry interrupted my thoughts.

"We're sorry for letting you grow up without parents," he told me. "but we had to let you live as a human. I could form a planet without a second thought, but have you ever tried to change a freaking diaper? Impossible. Regardless, we were determined to learn. After you were born, Mr. and Mrs. Malone, who had been disguised as a married couple for years, decided to adopt children to study."

"So that's why they had so many sniveling brats around." I rudely mentioned. "I'll be damned."

Rabbitskin loudly cleared his throat.

"Sorry," I whispered.

"Try and refrain yourself, sir," the apeman said. "Filthy language shouldn't be used by someone of your stature."

Rabbitskin sure did hate it when I cursed. Unlike myself, he was a true fucking gentleman.

Without warning, The Four walked straight over and placed their heads against mine. It made me feel uncomfortable at first, but then something strange happened — I began to see. I mean, really see. Years and years of time rushed through my vision.

The Godlings' knowledge was being shared with me. I saw their lonely, empty worlds, their struggles and their pain. I felt their thirst for knowledge and their unending need to know. In a flash, I knew their entire history. I was officially number Five.

When I finally came to my senses, Rabbitskin was teary-eyed and wonderstruck, kneeling in the middle of the cabin floor. What he'd witnessed had rattled him.

"You don't have to kneel to us," Harry reassured the apeman. "You've given us joy beyond words, and we owe you our utmost respect. Please stand. We have much to discuss."

Rabbitskin slowly got up and rubbed his swollen eyes. I almost felt sorry for him. He was trying hard to represent the Carnavorines, but he was a little outmatched.

"We still want to stick to the plan," Harry told Rabbitskin. "We'd like to travel to Rabistca and meet with your leaders and scientists. We want to work together to find the answer to the ultimate question that's plagued our two races forever."

"Forgive my stupidity, sir, but what is the ultimate question?" Rabbitskin asked.

The answer involuntarily spewed from my mouth.

"Where did the people in this room come from?"

The Four seemed surprised I knew what they were thinking; so was I. What was happening to me?

"Forgive me for stating the obvious," Rabbitskin said. "But you've had billions of years to figure this out. What makes you think you can solve this now? You should know this is well beyond the reach of the Carnavorines."

We'll never be able to solve this problem," Harry admitted. "But he can."

To my horror, Harry was pointing at me.

Everyone in the room was now staring at me.

How the hell could I figure this out, I thought? For God's sake, I didn't even know Harry had been play-acting for the past 10 years. For the first time, I thought Harry Fox was wrong.

"Please enlighten me, sir." Rabbitskin said.

"It's true, for now, I'm probably smarter than my son." Harry told the apeman. "But remember, it took for me an eternity to obtain such knowledge. Logan is only 26-years-old and he's about to pass us all. We've been watching him closely and his potential is limitless. By our calculations, he'll probably exceed our knowledge by month's end, maybe even sooner. It took me a billion years to fully understand Foxtronics, and another billion to harness the Power of Zero. Logan learned it all in a few weeks. I couldn't teach you this in a thousand years."

"Logan is the link," Mrs. Malone solemnly stated. "He's the answer. He'll soon teach us things we can't imagine."

Mrs. Malone's statement got me thinking.

The Maze-O wasn't made for humans or the Carnavorines. The Maze-O was merely a way to test me and find out my potential. That's why Harry wasn't interested in the company, and why I was left to run things alone. These immortals weren't worried about keeping Foxtronics a secret. Nobody would ever understand it and they knew it. When I discovered telepathy, they'd seen enough, so had the Carnavorines.

Harry knew this would bring us all together, The Four; me, and the Carnavorines.

Now I understood.

Harry wasn't the chosen one — I was.

Chapter 10

It's midnight, only eight hours until my execution. It's quiet this time of night. Even the crazies have to sleep sometime. Most of the day I can hear their screams and moans out in the hallway. Unlike me, the rest of these circus freaks deserve to be here. These are the kind of whackos hardcore drugs are designed for. Sometimes I feel like hanging myself just to get away from these losers. I hate this shithole.

Henry is the only exception. He's the night watchman, appointed to stand guard outside my door so I don't escape. I like Henry. He talks to me and it helps pass the time.

I'm not so fortunate during daylight hours. My days are spent with Dr. J. W. Sprinkles, a world-renowned shrink sent here to personally trick information out of me. What a joke. He's wasting his time. I tried telling the truth down at the police precinct months ago, but that's how I ended up here.

I know what's really going on. They want to know the secret of Liquid Memory and the Power of Zero before I'm strung up. Since they can't find Harry, the secret will die with me. They've tried everything short of waterboarding to get me to talk. Some folks are even pushing to have my execution stayed for that very reason.

If they only knew who I really was, they'd understand they're wasting their time. I mean, I am the son of immortals.

I bet you're asking yourselves the same question. I bet you're wondering if I really died at the gallows this morning. You'll know in due time, but first you need to know more. I told you from the beginning that the truth would be tricky. I hope this is finally sinking in.

I wish I could see your faces now. I bet you're shitting bricks. Are you feeling guilty for hanging me this morning yet? Be honest, I've only scratched the surface and there's already "reasonable doubt" creeping into your simple minds.

When I was arrested, I tried to tell the proper authorities the truth. I told them exactly what happened, and why I had to blow up Preotec. Nobody would listen to me. They all said I was a psychopath. I'd just saved their asses and they were treating me like Jack the Ripper.

Since nobody could find Harry, the cops insinuated I murdered him and buried him somewhere inside the forest. Since we both vanished at the same time, and people knew I'd gone to his cabin, the police assumed there was foul play.

I knew this would probably happen. That's why I secretly placed a Maze-O deep inside my head where it couldn't be found by their scanners. This is how you're able to hear my story. That's why you're hanging by a thread, shaking in your boots. You better be; you don't know the half of it.

Some of you don't understand what's at stake with my execution. The Maze-O will become extinct. Your fate, that's still up in the air. I did everything in my power to stop it, even gave my life.

Foxtronics and Liquid Memory will soon become a part of the past. Don't you fools get it? We never told anyone how we did it.

Here's some more bad news for you.

After the rest of this broadcast is complete, once you understand the whole truth, every Maze-O on the planet will be shut down. The Maze-O secretly implanted in my head will render them all useless. The mighty Maze-O will be no more. I hope you didn't throw away your old computers. Get ready to take a giant leap backwards.

You pathetic humans. You run around so self-absorbed and sure of yourselves. You're so confident in the reality you've created that you walk around with blinders on. You invent worthless gadgets to entertain yourself and carelessly play with them till the day you die, never reaching higher, never reaching further than your remote control.

Fools. For generations you've searched for answers, coming up with ridiculous ways to prove that your faith and convictions are absolute truths. You shun anyone who dares to question your beliefs, selfishly surrounding yourselves with like-minded followers. There's safety in numbers, and this gives you comfort, but now you're starting to learn what you really are — predictable lab rats, amusement for a superior race. Your short lifespans are meaningless and your possessions are merely silly trinkets with no real value.

I've got to stop. I'm letting my mind wander.

My hanging is drawing near and time is short.
Let's continue.

Chapter 11

Rabbitskin was eager to share this new revelation with his people, but he wasn't sure how the news would be received. The apeman wasn't merely bringing back two humans who'd lucked into some sort of new technology. He was bringing back the creators of the universe and one of their offspring.

This would answer many questions for the Carnavorines, but I sensed Rabbitskin was also feeling fear. Logically, if the Godlings could create worlds with little effort, they could also destroy them with ease. I must admit, I was thinking the same thing, and this scared the hell out of me.

It seemed to me, however, the Godlings and Carnavorines needed each other. The apemen needed planets to house their life-forms, and The Four desperately needed life to feed their lonely souls. I saw this as a match made in heaven, literally.

I excused myself and walked outside. I needed a moment to catch my breath, a moment alone.

Once outside, I tried to clear my head. All the hopes and dreams of The Four had been shown to me. Their long history was passed to me instantaneously. I wondered if I was an immortal, too.

To be honest, I didn't want any of this — none of it!

It was hard enough running the largest company on the planet. Now Harry and the Carnavorines were looking to me for answers to impossible questions like, who made them? How was I supposed to know? I didn't want to know.

As these questions filled my head, the sun began to peek through the trees. For some reason the daylight was a welcome sight and the warmth of a new day gave me peace.

Harry walked outside. He wanted a minute alone with me. I, however, was in no mood for a heart to heart with daddy. Don't get me wrong, I always looked up to Harry as a father figure, but I didn't appreciate being lied to all those years. It would've been nice to be raised by my real parents. I can't believe he abandoned me.

"You gonna be alright?" Harry asked, sitting next to me.

"Just soaking it all in," I said.

Harry and I sat in silence, stared at the forest, and watched the sun rise higher. It suddenly dawned on me why Harry spent so much time in the wilderness. After spending an eternity in total nothingness, this had to be paradise to him. I felt his loneliness when The Four touched me. Oddly, I also felt something else. For some reason, Harry felt isolated from the other three Godlings. I didn't understand this, but I'd help him if I could. After all, he was my father and the only friend I'd ever had.

Harry broke the long silence.

"I know this is difficult to absorb all at once. But join us, Logan. Together, we can accomplish great feats."

My answer surprised both of us.

"The Four have always looked for answers from the outside, even creating new worlds for the sole purpose of finding new places to look. This is why you fail. The world is a circle. You should know this because you taught it to me. Think about it. The Power of Zero is what brought us here and that's where we'll find the solution. You've been looking on the outside of the Circle, but what you seek lies within."

Where in the hell did that come from, I thought to myself?

Harry looked at me and smiled. "It has begun," he said.

My father was right. It had begun.

I didn't know how, but I was growing smarter by the minute. How smart? I began to understand anything I could imagine. Something must've happened when The Four touched me. I was somehow kicked into overdrive.

As we returned back inside the cabin, everyone began to monitor my every move. All of a sudden, I was being treated differently. I think Rabbitskin was even afraid of me now. I needed to lighten the mood.

"So, whose spaceship are we going to take to Rabistca?" I asked. "Hope one of them has a hot stewardess."

Rabbitskin and Harry let out a small chuckle, but no one else seemed amused.

"If it's alright with you fine people," Rabbitskin said. "I'd be honored to use your aircraft. I'm sure it's far superior to mine."

"We used to fly aircrafts much like the Carnavorines," Ben said. "But we're much more advanced now. We can arrive at Rabistca in a couple of days, maybe sooner."

"Why use a spaceship?" I said. "Space travel is possible without using aircrafts."

There I went again. My mouth was no longer attached to my brain and seemed to speak at will. I had uncontrollable runaway mouth syndrome.

"How's that possible?" Rabbitskin said.

The Four seemed interested to know as well.

"Cosmic rays," I replied. "They're undetectable by the human eye. As you know, light can be bent. Even humans possess this technology. However, if you could make a machine that could fold light, amazing things could be possible. With enough power, one could advance this folding process past the speed of light. With proper calculations and precision timing, a cosmic ray could be formed. Through Harry's formulas, this ray could be pointed to any coordinates in the universe. The ray would only last a few seconds but would transport any object inside the tube in a blink of an eye. I'd have to do some math, but I believe this theory would also work between alternate universes my father created."

The room went silent; I mean, dead air. The Four were completely taken by surprise and Rabbitskin's hairy jaw was nearly dragging the floor.

"Or, we could take Harry's ride," I said.

How was I coming up with this shit? It was safe to say that nobody cared about the Maze-O anymore. With every word that came out of my new-and-improved motor mouth, it was being pushed further onto the back burner.

From here on out, I needed to be careful with my words, more like Harry. He'd taught me that with the Maze-O. It's not always good to show your hand. Not to mention, I was surrounded by proven liars and tricksters, Gods with the gift of gab and masters of sleight of hand. Who knew what really awaited for me on Rabistca. Until I could figured out who was who, I was going to keep my big mouth shut. This wouldn't be easy for me. It wasn't in my nature.

After the initial shock from my cosmic ray comment wore off, The Four focused all their energy on questioning Rabbitskin. For some reason, they were more interested in him than I. Even as smart as I was becoming, it was only the Carnavorines who could produce life-forms. This technology baffled them, and they needed to know how.

For the next hour Rabbitskin was hammered with one question after another. With each new question, he appeared to become more uncomfortable. Being the well-mannered spokesman that he was, he politely explained this, and it was decided to save these questions for a more suitable time.

Everyone had been up for days, so we decided to stay for a night at the cabin and leave in the morning. It was always interesting to me that the Carnavorines needed sleep just like the humans and animals they'd created; food too. They'd somehow created humans to share their own needs. Hell, when Rabbitskin went to bed that night, he even snored like a chain saw.

Unlike the Carnavorines, the Godlings needed no sleep, food, nor water, but it didn't stop them. They loved the pleasures humans had created and enjoyed exploiting all of them, especially eating, and alcohol. I finally understood why Harry could eat so much and stay so damn skinny.

Being his son, I wondered if I needed food or water. Maybe I'd merely used them out of habit. Either way, I wasn't willing to give up a good pint of whiskey or a fat T-bone. Matter of fact, if I was immortal, that might be my new daily diet.

After everything had quieted down, I walked outside and laid down on a picnic table beside the horse barn. My head was hurting from the day's events. Whether I needed it or not, I fell asleep under the stars.

I was rudely awakened by Harry frantically shaking me by the shoulders. To my horror, I awoke inside Harry's lab on Maze Island.

"What the hell is going on?" I said. "Where am I?"

"You're in the same place you were five minutes ago." Harry told me, laughing. "I'm sorry. but I wanted to show you the power of the Maze-O. I put a 10-year fantasy program inside your head to show you where we could ultimately take this. Did it all seem real?"

"What day is this?" I said in a panic.

"Logan." Harry replied. "I met you yesterday. Just relax. I wanted to show you the potential of my new invention. Are you convinced? Do we have a winner?"

Chapter 12

"Logan! Logan! Logan!" Harry shouted. "Wake up. Wake up."

"What?" I moaned, struggling to open my eyes.

I told you earlier that I rarely dream. I guess this was one of those times. I was relieved when I realized I was still outside Harry's cabin. Thank God it was only a horrible nightmare.

It was becoming more difficult to keep up with the events that were changing by the minute. The last thing I needed was some freakish nightmare clouding my thoughts. I mean, this dream felt real, and the thought of my Maze-O being programmed to screw with my head was unsettling. Harry could've done this you know.

With that being said, going forward, I needed to know what I was seeing, and feeling was real. In short, I wanted my Maze-O removed, immediately! We didn't have the proper equipment, but Harry agreed to rig up something.

To tell the truth, I didn't need my Maze-O anymore. My intelligence was now light years from the information programmed into Harry's invention. After my unusual dream, I was glad to get rid of it.

The Four found it puzzling that I could dream at all. I had obviously adapted a few human traits. Why, was anyone's guess. Since I wasn't biologically related to humans in any way, it didn't seem possible. It even left Rabbitskin scratching his overgrown dome.

At first, when I revealed my nightmare, everyone got a kick out of it. The more they thought about it, though, the more it made them nervous. With that being said, by the end of the day, no one had their Maze-O attached. They'd all been removed. I guess my dream was a little too real for everyone.

Believe it or not, Harry had two Maze-Os, one over each temple. Figures; I didn't ask.

I didn't dwell on the nightmare for long. I was too excited about the trip to Rabistca, not to mention anxious to see Harry's secret aircraft. Rabbitskin was, too. We'd been chatting inside the cabin for a couple of hours when I began to grow agitated.

"Let's get this show on the road, Harry. We've yapped enough. Let's be on our way."

"We are on our way," Harry said. "We're already well beyond the Milky Way galaxy heading toward Rabistca."

"How's that, sir?" Rabbitskin questioned.

"Take a look out the window." Harry said.

Rabbitskin and I ran over to the window and eagerly pulled back the curtains. Astonishingly, Harry's cabin was zooming through space faster than words can say.

Streaks of blurry lights passed across my vision. An array of bright colors and speeding stars came and went in an instant. There were no controls, wings, nor a cockpit. The cabin was flying through the universe in absolute silence. Neither me nor Rabbitskin knew until we were told.

Harry walked over to Rabbitskin, who was still gawking out the window in disbelief.

"I know this is bizarre," he told the apeman. "After all these years we can make just about anything fly. Maybe in due time we could've taught the Carnavorines this method of travel. But after listening to Logan's Cosmic-ray spiel earlier, we don't need to worry about this soon to be out-dated technology. Now please excuse me, The Four must concentrate to move us safely to our destination."

Harry walked over and joined the other Godlings. They were all sitting side by side with their heads touching and appeared to be in a trance.

The Four had been traveling through space for an eternity, so I was pretty sure they knew what they were doing. Matter of fact, I knew exactly what they were doing and how they were doing it. I kept this information to myself. I'd made a promise to keep my mouth shut. Plus, I didn't want to worry Rabbitskin. He didn't look so good.

I thought this might be a good time to get to know Rabbitskin a little better. Maybe it would help ease the tension. Sure, the cordial Carnavorine seemed polite enough, but I wanted to know what he really thought about all this crazy shit. It was time to find out, time to pick his brain.

Rabbitskin was still glued in place. Stuck, looking out the window.

"It's funny," he finally said. "Even as advanced as my people are, when we fly, we still need spacesuits to sustain proper oxygen levels and temperature control. Yet, here we are breathing easily, and the temperature inside this flying cabin is perfect."

Rabbitskin began to weep.

"What's wrong?" I asked.

"My arrogance."

"Arrogance?"

"The Carnavorines are a proud people," he said, sniffing. "We've been so confident in our own accomplishments that we didn't see the big picture. We observe our creations as though we're gods. But we're not gods. You are. Our egos have been unwarranted and our over-confidence, appalling. Standing before you, I feel ashamed."

Rabbitskin fell to his knees.

"Please forgive me, sir."

I'd never been inside a church, but this must be what a priest felt like inside his confessional. Rabbitskin was confessing and somehow looking to me for penitence. It made me feel weird and I didn't know what to do. I wasn't in the Bigfoot forgiveness business. Should I tell him to give me three hail monkeys or what? This was confusing.

It was now becoming apparent that humans had adopted the exact same emotions as their creators. Rabbitskin was an emotional creature and proudly wore his feelings on his sleeve. I really liked that about him. He was someone I could relate to, someone willing to share himself.

As for the Four, sure, they were likable enough, but they were closer to well-oiled machines than humans. Don't get me wrong, Harry had always been a perfect gentleman, but there was something missing. There was no love, hate, or affection. It was more like redundant politeness and carefully thought out political correctness. It was nearly impossible to detect, but no doubt, rehearsed for millions of years.

This is what the Godlings had been missing all these years. The Carnavorines had plenty of emotions and graciously embedded it into all their creations. The Four only imitated it; copied it to perfection. They didn't understand it any more than they understood how to create life-forms.

My guess was that The Four longed for it. It meant more to them than they were letting on. Could this be the reason I was conceived? Was I merely an experiment?

Even my mother, Mrs. Malone, hadn't shown me any real motherly love since she revealed herself to me. At the same time, I didn't feel any love for her either. I guess you can't give what you don't get. It was a lot to think about.

Harry had play-acted his part perfectly without any remorse or regret. He'd fooled me and Rabbitskin right up to the end, pretending to be so frightened when he told his tale of Bigfoot. He could've won an Academy Award for that performance — best supporting actor in a horror film. The Four all played a part in this elaborate scheme, and my dumbass never saw it coming.

I still didn't know everything, but I knew one thing for certain. I felt more of a connection to Rabbitskin than the Godlings. This confused me because I had no link to the gentle giant. I was in no way related to the Carnavorines or a direct descendant of any species they'd created. This was a piece of the puzzle I'd have to solve.

I'd been so deep in thought that I'd completely forgotten about Rabbitskin, who was still on his knees next to me.

"Please stand." I said. "You have nothing to apologize for."

I looked over at The Four. They were obviously going to be busy for the rest of the trip. They were still huddled on the couch deep into their trance. My cosmic ray idea would've worked better. We would be there already. Oh well, I needed some quality time with Rabbitskin anyway.

We walked over and I sat at the kitchen table. Rabbitskin perched his oversized butt on top of the table again.

"Have you contacted your superiors with news of our arrival?" I asked the apeman.

"Yes sir, but as I've mentioned before, our communication system is slower than we'd like. My message should reach Rabistca before we arrive. To be honest, I don't know how it'll be received. Maybe they'll think I've lost my bloody marbles."

"I'm sure it'll be difficult at first," I said. "But if your leaders are as hospitable as you, we'll have no problems."

"Thank you, sir," the apeman said. "I'll assure you, your family will be treated as royalty while on Rabistca."

Family? The word itself threw me for a loop. I'd never had a family before. I looked over at my newly discovered kinfolk, all huddled together.

I wish I could've taken them to Parents Day back in pre-school ...

"So, little Logan," the teacher would say, "please explain to the class what your parents do."

"They're immortals," I'd respond. "In their spare time, they stick their heads together and fly log cabins around alternate worlds. Now, can I be excused? I have to go do a number two, which is the square root of four."

My mind was wandering; too much information in a short amount of time. I had to pull it together. I needed to refocus on Rabbitskin. Who knows, this could be the last time I'd be alone with him.

"What's Rabistca like?" I asked.

Rabbitskin's demeanor instantly lightened when I asked him this simple question. It had been a long time since he'd seen his home planet. Although the circumstances were a bit unusual, he had to be anxious to return home.

"It's been 600 years since I've seen it," he recalled. "But I can still smell the Wind-Daisies that bloom in Pine Valley every blue lunar cycle."

Rabbitskin sniffed the air as though he was already there. He was remembering.

"Our planet is divided into three sections, Forest, Desert, and Ocean. Unlike Earth, our three environments are completely separate from one another. The ocean wraps around our planet in the center and divides the forest and desert portions that lay on each side. Each is equal in size and area. We still use our planet as a testing ground for new and old species alike. Remember, sir, the Carnavorines are not only masters of producing life-forms, but livable environments, as well. We arranged our planet this way for good reason."

I was all ears. I was the only one inside the flying cabin who had never seen another planet. This was exciting for me.

"Please," I begged. "Tell me everything. Don't stop."

"As scientists," he continued, "we spend our entire lives studying in one of the three terrains. I'm from the forest side of the planet. That's where all the Humanologists live. When we're born, our King, Babbleskin, decides which of the three terrains newborns will spend their lives. Once this is decided, that's the final word. Only the leaders from the three terrains can talk among themselves and share knowledge. As a general rule, we're not allowed to visit the sections we're not assigned to. This would prove to be a distraction and could affect our work. Work comes first on Rabistca. We fully understand the great responsibility that comes with what we do. I can assure you, sir, we don't take it lightly."

"How does your King have the time to personally assign each and every newborn?" I questioned. "It doesn't seem possible."

"You're assuming our planet is as populated as Earth." Rabbitskin said. "But it's not. There's only 1,111 of us. There's never any more or any less. It's always the same. When one dies, another is born. Males are replaced by males and the same goes for females. Unlike humans, childhood doesn't exist for Carnavorines. Only hours after birth, we become full-grown adults who instantly possess the full knowledge and knowhow of our ancestors. Our abilities derive from instinct, no different than the animals back on your planet."

Rabbitskin paused as if he was trying to figure out a way to better explain himself.

"Don't you see, Logan," he finally said. "That's why The Four can't learn our skills. Instinct is given at birth and can't be learned through theories or math. Even as smart as you're becoming, sadly, you'll never obtain this knowledge. Unfortunately, you have to be born with it."

It had been a while, but my mouth began to shoot off again. This was becoming a reflex reaction that I obviously couldn't control.

"1,111 is the number that balances all life," I involuntarily said. "For example, if you could lay out your anatomy flat on a piece of paper and mark a dot on all the axis points, they'd number exactly 1,111. One more or less, the axis would be unbalanced, and life couldn't exist. The same could be said about any given species' DNA. If you look deep into the micros of a DNA strand, you'd find the real make-up of organisms, Cell-Straps. Cell-Straps are the genesis of all things and are also made up of 1,111 particles. If this is true, which it is, the Carnavorines would have to keep an exact population of 1,111, not only to create life, but to keep it perfectly balanced. It wouldn't work any other way. To you, instinct has always been an indescribable emotion instilled into a creature at birth. To me, it's simple math."

I don't know who was more shocked by what I had just said. I could've gone on for hours in great detail, but why waste my breath. It was over my furry friend's head. I do think, however, that this was the straw that broke the Yeti's back. Rabbitskin began to fully realize who I was becoming, and the words of Mrs. Malone rang loudly in his ears — Logan is the link. He's the answer. He'll soon teach us things we can't imagine.

At that point, we were both ready to accept the truth. My fate was sealed, my future set. I knew I couldn't stop it, but I did want to control it. Rabbitskin and I both accepted it on that day, and there was no need to discuss it any further.

I couldn't worry about it any longer. Solving the world's problems would have to wait. For now, I wanted to kick back and let my new friend tell me more amazing stories about his home planet.

Rabbitskin talked for hours. He was a master storyteller and could describe things in such wonderful depth. His love for the subject and steady, deep voice lured me deep into his world. His combination of sharp memories and impeccable wit drove the stories home as we sped toward the home he so dearly loved.

Chapter 13

The Maze-O dominated my life for 10 long years. Now it seemed petty and obsolete, a wasted decade. Worst of all, my tunnel vision had made me blind. I'd left my flanks unguarded. It wouldn't happen again. Now I was a little wiser to the game. When The Four touched me, they unleashed a beast, an unstoppable brain juiced up on the good stuff; a cerebrum freak.

I suddenly felt the strange sensation that I was being watched. I jerked around to see The Four standing directly behind me.

"We're here," Mr. Malone said, in a robotic tone. "We've made good time and have arrived sooner than anticipated."

I ran over to the window, and there was Rabistca.

I'll try and describe it, but it won't do it any justice. It would be like taking a picture of the Grand Canyon with a black and white Polaroid; some things you have to see for yourself.

Rabistca was probably a hundred times the size of Earth. It was gigantic. Rabbitskin had described it to a T. The planet was perfectly divided into three distinct sections.

The middle band, which was the ocean section, really stood out from our vantage point. Deep blues and rich greens intermingled until they formed a color that can only be described as breathtaking. There were no islands nor land masses within the well-defined borders of the sea. One could only wonder what mysterious creatures lurked in the deep regions beneath these bottomless, ancient waters.

The desert portion was an endless carpet of brown sand and sweeping barren rock. It was a dry, desolate wasteland that seemed to have no beginning or end.

Even from high above the planet, the lush forest section was a sight to see. Soon I would see it up close. Only then would I realize the magnitude of what I was looking at.

I quickly counted more than 20 moons, all different sizes and colors. Although the planet was well illuminated, I couldn't make out the source of light. As far as I could tell, there was no sun.

As we eased closer to the planet, the bigger it became and the smaller I grew. I was a kid in a candy store.

The Four walked to a window and glanced down at their planet. It was they who had created it, formed it out of nothing. They had to be elated at what the Carnavorines had done with it. It was a fine home make-over.

Mrs. Malone was next to speak, again in a unemotional manner.

"Words can't express the beauty the Carnavorines have brought to the universe," she said. "This planet was once a large floating rock, void of life. Now, it's a living and breathing wonder, filled with plants, animals, and many colorful things. We've waited millions of years for the right time, a day in which our two great races would finally meet. Today is that day. This truly is a glorious occasion."

The words of Mrs. Malone carried considerable substance, but I wasn't so easily convinced. I wasn't going to be tricked by mere words again. I'd hold my judgments until I could see the big picture. At this point, I was more interested in actions than fancy speeches.

"Where should we land?" Harry asked Rabbitskin.

"Our headquarters is just inside the Forest section, which is my home sector. We'll have to land on the beach along the forest's edge. The woods are too thick and grow too fast for building landing strips. Besides, it's forbidden to harm the vegetation that grows inside the woodlands. If my message got through, we should have a welcoming party there to greet us."

"It got through," I said.

"How do you know this sir?" Rabbitskin replied.

"Because your welcoming party is right outside the door."

Before Rabbitskin had finished his sentence, The Four had landed the cabin where he'd instructed. Their maneuvering abilities were 100% stealth in a split second. This is why I stayed close to the window whenever I could. It was the only way to find out where the hell I was at.

On the beach stood two large Carnavorines curiously looking over the cabin. After what I'd seen in the past few days, this didn't surprise me, but what they clutched in their hands did. Each apemen held a huge leash with a saber-toothed tiger fastened to the end. They were straight out of an ancient history book.

The gorgeous beasts were sitting by their masters with their broad chests bowed out. Each had razor-sharp tusks that protruded well below their massive jaws. Their muscular bodies were covered with thick, shiny fur that clung to their ripped frames like body armor. This was the first of many unusual animals that I'd likely encounter on Rabistca, but for the moment, I was completely enamored by their beauty.

Rabbitskin stormed out the front door. I almost expected him to scream for help, but he didn't. He jogged over and embraced his kinsmen and began exchanging pleasantries in a strange dialect. The language consisted of high-pitched shrieks and long-drawn-out whistles, the opposite of what I expected. They sounded like a bunch of tweety birds. I kept my opinion to myself.

Next, something crazy happened.

I began to understand what they were saying. I was learning their language as fast as they were speaking it. Oh hell no! Here we go again.

Please don't start whistling. Please don't start whistling, I begged myself. Of course, my mouth had other plans. I bolted out of that cabin chirping like a sparrow. I was walking down the beach whistling Dixie and couldn't make it stop.

"Williiip Wiiiiip wipp wiu wi," squawked from my puckered lips as I approached the three startled Carnavorines and their two prehistoric companions.

For those of you who don't talk bird, it basically means — nice kitty kitty. I wasn't worried about the Carnavorines, but up close, the tigers were twice the size of a full-grown male lion back home.

I kindly introduced myself to the two strangers and politely asked if we could continue our conversation in English. I had no intention of chirping anymore. Besides the fact that whistling sucks, my vocal cords couldn't sustain the punishment from the high-pitched sounds for much longer. They were already becoming quite sore.

During my unexpected promenade down the beach, The Godlings had followed close behind and were now standing right beside me. Rabbitskin's curious companions looked at each of us, sizing us up. Although they brimmed with confidence on the outside, I detected fear in each of them.

Harry introduced himself using the Carnavorines' native tongue. This didn't surprise me. The Four had been observing the apemen for millions of years. This was ample time for them to learn their unique language.

Later, Harry would tell me that the Carnavorine dialect had been almost impossible for them to learn, struggling for centuries with the bird-like sounds. All the years of practice didn't seem to help. Harry spoke with a heavy accent, and the tones were all wrong.

I wanted to help him as he fumbled through the difficult series of squawks, but he was trying so hard to be cordial. The Carnavorines just smiled and nodded. They couldn't understand a damn thing he was saying either.

At one point, Rabbitskin looked at me and winked. It was all I could do not to burst out laughing. Harry sounded like a chicken on crack. This was painful. Should I stop this, I thought? Rabbitskin beat me to the punch.

"We thank you, sir, for learning our native tongue," he told Harry. "But since you're our guest, we insist that we speak English while on Rabistca, this is the primary language of young Mr. Spencer and it'd be uncivil to do otherwise. We want to make you feel as welcome as possible. I can assure you that the Carnavorines are fluent in every known language of our colonized planets, human or animal. This will be no burden to us."

Rabbitskin's two companions were named Fellskin and Bowskin, the two cats, Yora and Tanjo. They'd been studying lifeforms near the beach when they'd been contacted by Babbleskin personally. He'd stressed that we were of immeasurable importance and were to be treated as such. Other than that, they had no idea who we were. The apemen had witnessed the cabin as it suddenly appeared on the beach, and they became frightened.

Fellskin was relieved after seeing Rabbitskin exit the cabin and was overjoyed to reunite with his old friend. Bowskin had only heard of him through Fellskin's never-ending stories and recollections, but they'd never met in person. Rabbitskin was obviously considered in high regard among his kinsman, and Bowskin was honored to be in the presence of such a renowned apeman.

Fellskin told us that the Carnavorine headquarters was a difficult two-day journey by foot, through many dangerous and unpredictable environments such as the Jimini Jungle. This untamed rainforest was heavily populated with a potpourri of wild creatures from different worlds and long-forgotten generations. The area was a breeding ground for plant and animals alike that were purposely allowed to run amok. This was the way of the Carnavorines. They created and observed. They never interfere.

Babbleskin had sent his apologies for not meeting us personally, but the message from Rabbitskin hadn't reached him in time. We were informed that there were no roads, buildings, or vehicles allowed in the Jimini Jungle. Their headquarters, a city named Sina, was built inside a massive cave, deep underground. This was where their King lived, and it also housed the main laboratory for their scientific endeavors.

All flying machines were stored deep in underwater caves near the ocean section of the planet. The same laws applied for each section. No structures were allowed on the surface. Absolutely nothing artificial could be built, driven or manufactured topside.

An ancient trail was the only way through the jungle. It wound itself through thick woodlands and deep canyons from Sina to the beach where we now stood. Even the Carnavorines were no match for the dangers that lurked off the beaten path. The trail was the only safe passage to Sina. This was made clear to us.

Fellskin told us about one of his friends, Sureskin, who was killed by a slyth, a vicious snake-like serpent with thousands of tiny legs and just as many teeth. Fellskin's sidekick had unwittingly strayed too far from the trail which had sealed his fate. Bowskin was Sureskin's replacement and had been his partner since. Remember, when one dies, another is born.

Anyway, I was officially scared shitless. The Four were proven immortals, but I wasn't. Cockroaches made me scream and cower in the corner. This was a nightmare.

Rabistca was the opposite of what I'd expected. I'd envisioned an elaborate city with multiple test animals in cages, kind of like a sleek, modern zoo-world. I didn't come here to be an appetizer for a slyth or whatever you call it, and I preferred animals with four legs, eight at the most; none for snakes.

I had to control my fear. For God's sake, I was the son of immortals. Besides, I couldn't act like a total pussy in front of a saber-toothed tiger.

"Don't worry, young Mr. Spencer," Rabbitskin said. "Yora and Tanjo will protect us. Their skills have no equal. Not even here."

"I'm not worried." I said.

I don't think anyone believed me. My poker face was pitiful.

My fears were real, but my curiosity, stronger. Excitement began to creep over every inch of my body. I could feel it in my bones.

An adventure was about to begin.

Chapter 14

I'd been so distracted by the introductions on the beach, I'd failed to notice the jungle looming over my left shoulder. While The Four were busy talking to the Carnavorines, I snuck over to get a better peek.

I'd seen the Redwood forest in a simulation booth when I was a kid, but nothing could prepare me for standing next to the Jimini Jungle. Redwoods would be considered twigs in this ancient maze of foliage.

An assortment of unfamiliar trees towered into the heavens, some disappearing high into the clouds. These monstrosities weren't confined to merely growing upward. They sprouted into hundreds of directions, each having freewill to roam where they may. Some traveled sideways while others plunged back into the ground, starting the whole process over again.

Every root, leaf, and branch were engaged in a continual battle for real estate in the overcrowded space available. The thick hardwoods were so intertwined, I couldn't tell where one started, and another began.

Countless flowers and colorful blooms sprouted from the jungle floor. Gigantic bees tirelessly flew from one to another, gorging themselves on the abundance of sweet nectar. As the happy insects playfully maneuvered for position, their steady hum filled the airwaves.

The intoxicating aroma seeping from the tropical forest was so powerful, it smelled like I was knee-deep in honeysuckles. I drew in long, deep breaths to allow the sugary fragrance to swirl through my senses.

Strange sounds culminated from deep within the entangled mass. Some I recognized as birds or frogs, but others were foreign to my ears. Together, they sounded like an orchestra, a symphony of harmony conducted by chance, yet perfectly choreographed through years of practice. They were a seasoned band.

Suddenly, the chatter was hushed by a resounding growl echoing through the underbrush. The deep grumble sent a cold shiver down the back of my neck. Thankfully, the silence didn't last long, and the band began to play again. This got my attention in a hurry. The Jimini Jungle was not to be taken lightly.

In every nook and cranny was a bounty of life. The jungle seemed to shift, move, flow like a mighty river. I gained strength from being close to it. Its energy poured through me, and I stood helplessly humbled, a scolded child.

No wonder the Carnavorines wouldn't allow man-made devices on the surface of their planet. How could anyone interfere with what occurred naturally in this holy place, this garden of magnificence?

This was why the Carnavorines let their creations do as they pleased. No plan nor scheme could ever duplicate this. Only through natural process could these elements come together so flawlessly. Each were different, but together they formed a unique mixture that could only be obtained by simply leaving them alone. The strong adapted; the weak were eliminated.

How disappointed the Carnavorines must've been with their greatest creation, Man. Standing beside the forest, I felt ashamed. I was guilty of being blind.

I recalled how Harry marveled over every tree, plant, and bug on our annual trip to the Global Wilderness Sanctuary. He didn't take life for granted like I did. What a fool I'd been.

Now I understood why the apemen kept such a careful eye on humans. While the Carnavorines were thoughtful environmentalists, humans were great destroyers with no conscience to speak of.

How sad it must've been for Rabbitskin, sitting in silence while Earth was turned into a concrete jungle, a cesspool filled with greedy takers and clear-cutting lunatics. For 600 years he stood idly by while thousands of wonderful animal and plant species vanished one by one, unable to act, powerless. Being a Humanologist was a thankless job.

The more I learned about the Carnavorines, the more I came to respect them. They embraced technology but didn't use it to destroy or foolishly replace other things. They had tons of power, but even more compassion, and that's what I loved most about them.

Later I was told the Carnavorines had created certain animals for the sole purpose of a food source. They'd only eat these specific items. Chickens, cows, pigs, and other domesticated animals not found on Earth were all on the approved-grub list.

Wild animals were strictly forbidden to be killed or harmed. Besides fish and a few other seafoods, wildlife was wildlife; only chance could decide their fate.

The one exception was self-defense. Naturally, if a species tried to harm a Carnavorine, the proper force could be used for their own protection.

I can't recall how long I stood there that day, but I can honestly tell you, I was reborn. Without saying a word, the Jimini Jungle had changed me forever.

Chapter 15

While I was daydreaming, I failed to notice Rabbitskin slipping up behind me. I almost jumped out of my skin when he unexpectedly tapped me on the shoulder.

"Careful, young Mr. Spencer," he whispered. "The Jimini Jungle is as deadly as it is beautiful. If you feel the need to be this close, you must be accompanied by a Protector."

"A Protector?" I said. "What's that?"

"Yora and Tanjo are Protectors," Rabbitskin explained. "And the Carnavorines aren't allowed near the jungle without them. Earth scientists named them saber-toothed tigers after finding their remains years ago. Humans were wise to study fossils, but old bones don't always tell the truth. There are many misconceptions back on Earth."

"Go on," I said. Now he had my attention.

"Protectors were incubated and grown millions of years ago by one of our ancient kings, Cowskin. His methods were unprecedented, and his formulas are still used today. Although his life was cut short, he gave us our greatest gift, the Protectors."

"What happened to him?" I asked.

"He was executed," Rabbitskin surprisingly said.

"For what?"

"Unfortunately, he broke our most sacred law," Rabbitskin replied. "Instead of releasing his creations to roam free and study, he secretly hid two in his royal chambers. You see, the kittens had grown so fond of their creator they didn't want to leave his side. This was the first time any species had done this. This confused Cowskin, but also touched his heart."

"So, what's the problem?" I said in disbelief.

"Failure to follow our most sacred law is punishable by death," the apeman warned. "Interfering in any way can't be allowed. There are absolutely no exceptions! Nonetheless, Cowskin's love for the kittens outweighed his logic, and he went to great lengths hiding his new friends. He needed more time to figure them out. Before he could complete his secret study, however, the kittens were discovered. Cowskin was executed the following day."

Could this possibly be true, I thought? How could a moral and compassionate race like the Carnavorines kill one of their own over such a harmless act?

"I can tell you're not pleased with our forefathers' decision," Rabbitskin said, noticing my concern. "But our most sacred law was written for a reason."

"But his only crime was love," I pleaded. "Wasn't there any other way?"

"We all love what we create, lad. There is no higher love. But we can't allow ourselves to selfishly hold on to our creations. Emotional attachment can only lead to attempted control, young Mr. Spencer."

"But look at the Protectors," I pointed out. "Are they not controlled? Fellskin and Bowskin have them on a leash. This is so hypocritical."

"No, sir," Rabbitskin said. "Believe it or not, the Protectors instinct is to serve and protect the Carnavorines. Cowskin was starting to figure this out. He also knew the most sacred law must be followed. It's what you humans call a Catch-22. Only after his death, when the Protectors had been observed for months, did we realize the sacred law hadn't been broken. Cowskin is still remembered today as an unselfish King who gave his life to protect our most sacred law."

Rabbitskin told me the Protectors had been dispatched to Earth during the Cenozoic era. There were 11 Carnavorines on our planet then, and numerous cats were sent to keep them safe. Sadly, these were dangerous times and many Protectors lost their lives saving their masters. Years later, when their fossilized remains were found, anthropologists naturally assumed the saber-toothed tigers were native to Earth.

I glanced over at Yora and Tanjo, obediently standing beside their masters. I began to see them in a whole new light.

Everything in this world was new to me, and I wanted to know more. I couldn't wait to see what was around the next corner.

Sometime during our conversation, Fellskin must've noticed how close Rabbitskin and I were to the jungle, much too close for his liking. The apeman rushed over to our position with Yora leading the way. He had strict orders from the King to keep us safe at all cost.

"We should go," he told Rabbitskin when he arrived. "We shouldn't leave the King waiting. Besides, I'm sure you'd love to see your old friend again."

"Yes," Rabbitskin agreed. "It's been many years since I've traveled the Perigon Trail. I've waited a long time for this day to come."

"Babbleskin has summoned the Council of Ten," Fellskin said, in a more official tone. "All leaders have been rushed to Sina for an emergency meeting at the Halls of Goya. Forest, Ocean, and Desert will each be represented, sir."

"The Halls of Goya?" Rabbitskin scoffed. "The Halls haven't been used for a million years. You know that. The Silver Stone has blocked the entrance for generations."

"It's a test," I blurted out.

By now, Rabbitskin had gotten used to my sudden outbursts, but Fellskin was shocked by my response. I was, too, because I was actually seeing a vision this time. I saw the Silver Stone and the Halls of Goya as if I were there in person. I saw everything, even the King, nervously awaiting our arrival.

I began to calmly recite what I'd seen.

"The Halls of Goya was a place where leaders gathered in the olden age of the Carnavorines. It was constructed deep underground, carved out of a single piece of pure Goya marble found in an abandoned cave. Everything was crafted from the green and silver marble, even the tables and chairs used by the Council. Giant columns lined the halls, each chiseled into shapes of different species the Carnavorines had created. It hasn't been seen in a million years, yet it just appeared to me clearly. It's the most magnificent place I've ever seen."

"This is a trick," Fellskin cried out.

"No," Rabbitskin assured his companion. "But it's not meant for your ears. Please join the others and prepare to leave. I need to talk to Mr. Spencer alone."

Fellskin slowly backed away as if he'd seen a ghost. Once he was out of hearing range, Rabbitskin resumed our conversation.

"I know your powers are growing stronger," he whispered. "But going forward, you must hold your tongue until we're in a more proper setting. Now with that being said, you mentioned something about a test?"

"As you well know," I said, "the Halls of Goya only had one way in, and one way out, the Grand Arch. Detailed replicas of time-honored kings were engraved into the arch and completely covered the marbled masterpiece. As a beacon of hope, it was polished for a thousand years and shined so brightly, it could be seen from miles away."

"But what do you know about the Silver Stone?" Rabbitskin said. "Where did it come from? Why was it placed there?"

"The Silver Stone has held the Halls of Goya captive for so long, it's almost become a myth." I continued. "It appeared out of nowhere; a form-fitting stone wedged snugly inside the famous entryway. For generations your people tried to drill it, blast it, crack it, or move it, but the mysterious rock couldn't be penetrated. It was determined by Carnavorine engineers that any attempt to bore around the Silver Stone would cause total collapse. After years of making no headway, the apemen finally gave up the fight. Their greatest architectural achievement was lost."

"It was Harry, wasn't it?" Rabbitskin growled.

"Yes."

"Why?"

"Hard to tell," I said. "But your king, Babbleskin, is going to use it as a test. A way of seeing if The Four are legit. The Silver Stone is from my father's home planet Lorivox and is made of Menite, the strongest mineral in all the known universes. I don't know how I know this. I just do."

Things were getting complicated. At this point, I didn't know whom to trust.

Chapter 16

Rabbitskin and I rejoined the others who had been impatiently waiting on the beach. We didn't say anything to them about my vision. Rabbitskin was right. These topics should be discussed at a more suitable place. It was time to get to Sina.

The Carnavorines led us down the shoreline for a couple of miles until we reached the beginning of the Perigon Trail. I was frightened at first, but after one quick look down the footpath, I was relieved. It was more like a tunnel than a trail.

The rounded walls were made from braided vines used to hold back the aggressive and ever-expanding jungle. The strangulating vines were so tightly interwoven only a few stems and leaves could squeeze past their relentless grip. These rare offshoots, however, were quickly smothered, leaving them helplessly dangling from the cracks, dead, dying from suffocation.

As we moved inside the cave-like trail, I noticed the vines gave off a glowing light. I walked over to investigate.

"They're shine-vines," Bowskin said, noticing my curiosity. "They grow on Morack Trees and are only found here on Rabistca. They have the strength of steel mesh and their glow never fades. They'll shield us from harm and light our path through the jungle, about a half day's walk. There we'll enter the Black Willow Swamp. That's where the real danger begins."

The Black Willow Swamp? The name itself made my skin crawl. This probably wasn't a place where cartoon animals lived, and I highly doubt we'd see Kermit the Frog happily playing a tune on his favorite lily pad. I more envisioned mosquitos the size of eagles and alligators as long as freight trains, all picking on the new guy. I tried not to think about it. We seemed safe for now.

The shine-vines were impressive. It was like walking through a well-lit botanical garden or groomed nature trail. Yora and Tanjo led the way with Bowskin and Fellskin firmly grasping their thick leashes. Rabbitskin and I walked directly behind the Carnavorines while The Four stayed close to our heels.

There was no talking at first, only the eerie sound of the Protectors sniffing and clawing the trail, and the haunting jungle-cries pouring through the tiny seams of the gripping vines. A few hours into our journey, everyone resumed talking again, but the chitchat was kept to a whisper. Better not take any chances alerting the predators I was convinced were just outside the apeman tunnel numbering into the thousands.

The Carnavorines had fabricated this organic passage only using materials native to the forest, keeping within the guidelines of their ancient laws and traditions. In many ways they reminded me of the Indians who roamed America years ago. Like the apemen, the Native Americans had respect for nature, a balance. That is, until the greedy white man lied to them, raped their land, and forced their religion down their throats.

Rabbitskin had been there to witness it all. He saw the slaughter and casually took notes. This couldn't have been easy, even for a Carnavorine.

The Indians tribes of Earth always had a special belief in Bigfoot. Sasquatch is mentioned in nearly all their writings and teachings. Since their races were somewhat alike, I'm sure Rabbitskin watched them intently over the years. That's probably why there were so many sightings of Bigfoot by different tribes.

The Four were keeping to themselves. They seemed genuinely interested in the shine-vines and rubbed their fingers against the bumpy surface as they moved along. I sensed conflict inside them. Something was wrong.

No one knew it yet, but Harry had removed the Silver Stone. I saw it while we were walking but kept it to myself. After a million years, the Halls of Goya was open for business.

The rest of our long stroll through the shine-vines was uneventful. There were no more visions or outbursts. I walked in silence. The noise outside no longer bothered me. I now had faith in the apeman tunnel. Unfortunately, the pleasurable hike was overshadowed by the thought of the dark path ahead. With each step, we were getting closer to danger.

After endless hours of walking, Fellskin held up his arm, signaling us to stop.

"The safety of the shine-vines will end soon," he warned. "The swamp is near. We'll rest here and have a bite to eat before we move on."

Fellskin and Bowskin were each wearing satchels made from an unusual leathery material. They were positioned on their right hip, held by thin straps thrown over their neck and shoulder. Honestly, they looked like man purses to me. I wanted to make a wisecrack, but decided it'd be in poor taste.

Fellskin pulled a handful of white nuggets from his pouch and passed them around.

"What's that?" I asked.

"Jerky," Rabbitskin said, pitching one into his mouth. "Made from the breast of a roos. Good stuff. Try a piece."

Bowskin tossed a handful of roos jerky onto the ground near Yora and Tanjo, and they quickly wolfed them down. The Four turned down the snack. For them, food was only for enjoyment, and this wasn't a good time to be selfish. I also declined.

As we sat with our backs resting against the shine-vines, I nervously glanced down the now dimly lit trail. There, a compressed, sinister sound reverberated through the dark opening with full force. The evil wind blew wearily across my face and the steady racket, which was only amplified by our position inside the tunnel, rang unyielding in my ears. I was terrified.

Harry came over and sat beside me. I was glad he wanted to talk. I needed something to take my mind off my overactive imagination.

"You're starting to see things, aren't you?" he whispered.

"Yes," I whispered back. "What's this all about?"

"We'll talk later," he said. "Whatever you're seeing, just keep it yourself."

Harry got up and joined the others.

What the hell was that all about? I thought. The Four seemed to be hiding something, but what?

Although these questions laid heavily on my mind, the violent disturbance coming from the swamp was more of an immediate concern. Every now and then, the heavy thud of something plunging into the water would drown out the chattering insects. Whatever it was, it sounded big, hungry, and hellish.

"How will we cross the swamp?" I cautiously asked. "Will we have to wade through?"

Fellskin and Bowskin started laughing.

"What's so funny?" I snapped.

"Forgive me, sir," Bowskin said. "But wading through the water would be an instant death sentence. You wouldn't last five seconds."

"The Black Willow Swamp has flourished beyond our control, young Mr. Spencer," Rabbitskin interjected. "The black willows have grown so thick they've completely choked out all light, and most swamp creatures no longer have eyes. But don't let that give you a false sense of security. They've evolved into skillful hunters that strike by the slightest sound, slithering their way around by feel and instinct. The sad truth is, sir, we have no idea what lives in the swamp anymore. Shine-vines are useless, and even the Protectors have no authority there. Quite frankly, it's the most dangerous place in the universe."

I didn't know what to say. I wasn't going to take another step without a better explanation than that. I was looking forward to seeing Sina, but oh well. I wasn't going into the swamp; no freaking way.

"Don't look so rattled," Rabbitskin said, giggling. "There's a safe passage."

"How?" I desperately asked.

"Just ahead is the Slanted Root," he explained. "It'll lead us to the top of the black willows. That's the only way to cross the swamp, young lad. The canopy is covered in Spanish moss, which will allow us to travel high above the danger. The moss has been growing and compacting there for generations and can easily support the weight of an elephant. Yora and Tanjo have scaled the Slanted Root many times. They'll carry us safely through."

I felt better after hearing what Rabbitskin had to say, I just hoped the Slanted Root was really wide. Falling into the mouth of an eyeless predator didn't have a nice ring to it.

"Let's mount up," Fellskin suddenly announced. "Harry, you and Logan can ride Yora. Ben, Mr. and Mrs. Malone will be on Tanjo."

In any other circumstance I'd have major reservations about riding a saber-toothed tiger, but in this case, it wasn't a bad idea. Besides, now I could just hold on for dear life. This I could handle.

The Carnavorines helped us onto the Protectors. I was placed in front where I promptly put a death grip around Yora's neck. Harry nestled up behind me and was told to lock his arms around my waist. The others were situated on Tanjo in the same manner. Once we were securely in place, we were given our marching orders.

"Trust the Protectors," Fellskin instructed. "Remain still and don't make a sound during the brief climb. We'll be right on your tails."

I turned around to see a big smile on Harry's face. He was actually going to enjoy this. Being immortal, he was in no real danger. Before I could say anything, the cat launched into the darkness.

I held tight while my Protector took an immediate giant leap up. My eyes were open, but they were useless. I couldn't see Yora, but I could hear her rapid heartbeat as she prowled upward, undulating her muscular frame in a crouched position. The blaring noise inside the swamp was overwhelming, but we moved in stealth. Silence was our cloak, and we wore it well.

Within minutes Yora had scaled the Slanted Root, and we were sitting on top of the black willows. Seconds later, Tanjo ripped through the canopy with the apemen close behind.

I shielded my eyes to adjust to the brighter conditions. We were free from the darkness of the swamp and the confinement of the shine-vines, and it felt good.

I tested my footing and tried to get my sea legs. Moving along the top of the Spanish moss was like walking on a sponge. I bounced up and down to reassure myself of its strength. It was soft but sturdy.

In the sky, I finally noticed the source of light for Rabistca. Their sun was much closer than Earth's but still looked small zooming through the upper atmosphere. Like a shooting star, it flew across the heavens in a blistering dash.

"It's a Supar," Harry said, looking upward. "It locks onto the gravitational field of a planet and rotates around it. It'll orbit a planet this size about every five minutes. Every two days or so, it slowly pulls away from its host planet, pushing hard against the boundaries of its gravitational limits. I call this the rubber-band effect. This is when nightfall occurs. But night is sparse here, only lasting four to five hours until the Supar pulls back again. These small suns are quite remarkable; I should've made more."

Fellskin clung to every word. He couldn't understand how the stranger knew so much. As far as he knew, these were the first humans to set foot on his planet. And what did Harry mean when he said, "I should've made more?"

"Please, Mr. Rabbitskin," Fellskin begged. "Who are these humans and why are they here?"

"Patience," Rabbitskin softly said, trying to calm his old friend down. "Soon you'll know, but only after the King and Council have met in private. Until then, our guests are to be treated with respect. Please don't push this further."

"Of course, sir," Fellskin said, toning it down. "I humbly apologize if I've offended your guests or overstepped my boundaries."

Fellskin's assignment was to get us to Sina, not to ask questions. Rabbitskin reminded him of this in his usual courtly manner, but he was fully aware not to ask again.

"Let's keep moving," Rabbitskin said. "It's a long walk to the Canyon Wall. The Protectors need rest and water. Just beyond the wall, the West River flows. We'll make camp there."

This sounded like a good plan. Although we were high above the danger, the chaos inside the swamp could still be heard filtering up through the moss. I was ready to get this part of the journey over with.

The trip across the canopy was awkward. Walking on the mushy moss was like trudging through deep snow, and it wasn't long before my calves began to ache.

The Protectors were no longer on high alert, strolling alongside their masters with tails wagging. I took this as a good sign, especially since the two uptight Carnavorines were letting them walk without their leashes.

I'm sure the apemen hated making them wear the uncomfortable collars, but these cats were still young. Sometimes the younger cats were overprotective. As they matured, Protectors were weaned from their restraints, but Yora and Tanjo's time had not yet come.

At last, in the distance, a tall shape began to appear. I was hoping we were getting close to the West River. I was now struggling with the spongy surface, and my legs felt like boat anchors. As we neared the end of the swamp, I could see the Canyon Wall in all its glory.

Millions of building-sized boulders were neatly stacked, each fitting together like a perfect puzzle. Each stone had its own unique shape, size, and color, but they all shared the same purpose; building a masterpiece.

There was no telling how high this configuration stretched. A thin, smokey mist clutched the rock formation, and its peak was nowhere to be found. The black willows grew thick along the Canyon Wall, pushing hard against its rough surface.

On one hand, I couldn't stop admiring its beauty, but on the other, I wondered how we'd scale this seemingly impassable structure. I wasn't a mountain climber and, unless someone could shit a rope, we seemed to have walked into a dead end.

While I was looking over the Canyon Wall, Rabbitskin tapped me on the shoulder and pointed to narrow crevice in the middle of a large boulder.

"I believe that's what you're looking for, sir," he said. "We call it the Slender Gap. It leads to the West River."

The Spanish moss nosed its way deep inside this tiny fracture, providing a natural bridge to our next destination. Fellskin was giving us instructions on how to safely cross the mossy bridge when it happened!

From out of nowhere, something punched through the canopy in front of me. My worst nightmare had come true. A slyth had found a weak point near the mossy bridge and was waiting for some unexpected prey to pass. That unexpected prey was us.

Like an overgrown cobra, the snake-like creature rose 20 feet into the air. It hissed, fully exposing hundreds of razor-sharp teeth. With the speed of a cheetah, the slyth snapped down and swallowed Harry whole.

Yora and Tanjo leaped into the air, each latching onto the reptile's throat. The creature violently shook, trying to free itself, but it did little good. The cats dug their massive tusks deep into their adversary's windpipe, choking off its oxygen supply. Soon the serpent came crashing to the ground.

Fellskin walked over to the slyth, who was lying stationary inside a mossy trench. The beast was clearly deceased. Its eyes had popped out of their sockets and blood poured from its motionless mouth.

"Wo wi wee whop wo wo wor," Fellskin shrieked, calling off the Protectors.

Panting and out of breath, the victorious cats returned to their master's side.

"Is everyone alright?" Rabbitskin screamed.

"Yes," a familiar voice answered from behind us.

I whipped around to see Harry standing on the mossy bridge, unharmed and in one piece.

"How can this be?" Bowskin shouted. "I saw you swallowed by the beast. I saw it with my own two eyes."

"It's okay," Rabbitskin said, holding out his hand.

I walked over to check on Harry.

I knew my father was immortal, but actually seeing proof of it was shocking. The Godlings looked human, but they were more spirit than flesh.

Eerily, Ben and the Malones showed no emotions during the whole ordeal. Maybe they didn't feel like pretending anymore. Maybe this was the real them.

Suddenly, I had another vision. It was the Four. They were jealous. I was sure of it, but this wasn't fake, it was real. They wanted what the Carnavorines had. They wanted it bad. This wasn't good.

Chapter 17

The Carnavorines carried no knives, spears, or weapons. They didn't need to. The Protectors were killing machines. The slyth wasn't aware of this until it was too late. Last mistake he ever made.

I walked over to Yora and Tanjo and began gingerly stroking their necks. It was my way of thanking them. Their tusks were covered in blood, and Yora had a deep wound across her back. I began to baby talk them using their native tongue. They closed their eyes and softly purred.

"They're fond of you," Fellskin said in disbelief.

"I don't understand this," Bowskin declared, watching me pet the cats. "But I trust their instincts more than the King himself."

To my surprise, both apemen bowed at my feet.

Rabbitskin smiled at me and seemed pleased. The Four, however, gave me that creepy feeling again. I sensed more jealousy. I needed to talk to Harry.

"We must go," Rabbitskin insisted. "Slyths sometimes work in teams."

That's all I needed to hear. Check please. We scurried across the mossy bridge, and in single file, began to ease our way through the Slender Gap. Yora and Fellskin led the way, but this time Bowskin and Tanjo stayed in the rear to watch our backs.

Thankfully, the trip through the tiny passage was brief. The confined space made me feel claustrophobic. I was relieved when I began to hear the welcoming sound of water flowing. As the rush of water got louder, the canyon crevice grew smaller until we had to forcefully squeeze ourselves through. This was particularly brutal for me, but I finally shoved my way to the end.

I took pleasure knowing the Slender Gap was too small for a slyth to cram trough, and I prayed the horrors of the Black Willow Swamp were behind us for good.

Once we were through the passage and had regrouped, I took a look around.

A raging river flowed just beneath us, hugging the Canyon Wall as far as the eye could see. We quickly became damp from the constant spray rising up from the rocks below. An ancient fallen tree formed a sturdy bridge over the rapid waters providing easy access to the far bank. Generations of extra-large feet had pounded the river crossing until it had worn flat and smooth across the top. The old tree trunk had long petrified into stone, and I marveled over its rugged antique look.

Beyond the river was a lush forest of tall pines and hardwoods. Recognizable chirps and customary calls came from all directions. This was a friendly place; a place of rest.

"Do you identify with any of this?" Rabbitskin asked me.

"I think so," I replied.

"This is where I worked and studied for years," he said. "It's our prototype environment used on many planets, including yours. This is the Universal Forest, our most successful terrain."

We scampered across the petrified tree and made camp on a grassy bank at the river's edge. For ages, this spot had been a popular campsite for weary Carnavorines traveling up and down the Perigon Trail.

As I took a seat on the grass, Rabbitskin nonchalantly walked to the river, kneeled, and dipped his arm deep into the water. I didn't know what he was doing. Washing his hands was my best guess.

After a few seconds, he jerked his arm out and flung a large trout onto the bank. The fish jumped up and down gasping for air. As I got up to investigate, another landed beside the first. Within minutes, there were trout flipping and flopping all over the damn place. This wasn't just a place to rest; this was an intergalactic honey hole.

Harry and I ran over to gather the catch. We'd fished many times together in the past, but never like this. In my opinion, Rabbitskin was the world's greatest fisherman, and it was plain to see how he'd survived on Earth all those years.

It was good to see Harry playfully corralling the trout. It seemed to rekindle an old spark in him, and thankfully, he briefly became his old self again.

"Could've used Rabbitskin on Maze Island," he shouted, holding up the biggest fish.

"No doubt," I said, displaying a respectable trophy myself.

When Rabbitskin was done fishing, he joined his two kinsmen who had long disappeared into the woods. He and Bowskin soon returned with their arms full of firewood. They only gathered what was dead and laying on the ground, keeping within the guidelines of their ancient laws.

When Fellskin returned, he was surprisingly holding a big bouquet of white flowers.

"Awww, you shouldn't have," I jokingly said.

"They're not for you," he grunted. "They're for Yora."

Rabbitskin rescued me from the uncomfortable situation.

"Pickle Daisies have special healing powers, young Mr. Spencer. We plant them throughout the forest for times such as these. They can be pulled while still alive, but only in certain circumstances. They're the only flower on the approved list. All others should be enjoyed in their natural state. Not selfishly plucked, stuffed into a dirty vase, and left to wither and die."

There was a lesson in Rabbitskin's words, and I heard it loud and clear.

Fellskin walked to the river and dunked the daises into the water. When he pulled them back out, they had morphed into a dark green slimy goop. The Carnavorine began kneading the slime until it formed a large gooey ball.

Yora walked over and stood close to Fellskin. She'd been in many fights and understood exactly what this meant. The apeman gently rubbed the soothing substance onto her back, pushing it deep into her wound. She closed her eyes in relief as the Pickle Daises worked their magic.

After Yora was tended to, the Protectors were thrown the two biggest fish from the pile. They happily laid on their bellies grasping them with their front paws. Unlike the roos jerky, they'd take time to savor every bit of this rare delight.

The Carnavorines gathered some loose stones, formed a fire pit, and neatly stacked the firewood in the center. Bowskin pulled a small pebble from his satchel, tossed it into the pit, and the wood burst into flames.

Without saying a word, the three Carnavorines walked back into the forest and out of sight.

I didn't know how long the apemen would be gone, but for the first time since revealing their true identities, I was alone with The Four. They'd been suspiciously quiet since we'd left Earth, and this was a perfect opportunity to find out why.

I figured it wouldn't be long before the apemen returned so I didn't beat around the bush.

"I'm having visions," I announced to the group.

This perked the Godlings up. They became rabid dogs, foaming at the mouth.

"What about the Carnavorines?" Mrs. Malone said. "Can you learn their secrets?"

"The Green Houses," Mr. Malone jumped in. "Tell us what you've seen inside the Green Houses."

"Can you see the future?" Ben boldly asked.

"If there's something you know, tell us," Harry begged.

Something wasn't right here. The Four were making me feel uncomfortable with their cold interrogation tactics.

"I need more time," I said, playing dumb.

Until I could figure this out, my lips were sealed.

Thankfully, the apemen were already out of the woods heading our way. When they arrived at camp, they were each carrying huge gobs of red clay. I jumped up to greet them to remove myself from the tense situation.

"What's that for?" I asked.

"Come here and I'll show you," Rabbitskin said, waving me over to the stockpile of fish. I strolled over to the three Carnavorines to get a better look.

I watched intently while the apemen patted chucks of clay around each trout, entombing them inside. Once this was done, they threw them over the red-hot coals. In no time, the clay would harden and easily pull apart. The trout would be perfectly baked inside.

Whether we needed it or not, we all ate our share. It was even better than Ben's famous smoked mackerel. The Carnavorines had several fish each and seemed happy to be eating something besides dried meat for a change. Roos jerky was good survival food, but nothing like fresh trout. The feast lasted for hours until every bone was licked clean.

After dinner, we stretched out on the soft grass to relax. The next thing I heard was the thunderous sound of three Bigfoots snoring. What a racket. They snored like bears and talked like sparrows. Those Carnavorines were a strange bunch.

Yora and Tanjo had curled up near the fire and were also enjoying a nap. Ben, Mr. and Mrs. Malone sat shoulder to shoulder and went into some sort of weird trance.

Once everyone was asleep, I went over and poked Harry.

"Hey," I whispered, pointing to the river. "We've gotta try."

"Let's do it," Harry said, grinning ear to ear.

We eased down to the river's edge, rolled up our sleeves, and tentatively placed our hands into the icy water. Like a couple of morons, we kneeled there for hours with our numb arms in the river, feeling around, but we caught nothing.

Demoralized, we snuck up the bank and laid back down on the grass. Later, when Rabbitskin awoke, I told him nothing. Being outfished by an overgrown ape was something I was definitely going to keep to myself.

Everyone slept while Harry and I laid on the grassy bank gazing at the sky. Darkness had fallen on Rabistca. The rubber-band effect was in full swing. High above, the Supar, which now looked like a dimly lit star, shot across the sky time and again. Each time it passed, its reflection revealed the planet's many colorful moons. We didn't sleep a wink. We couldn't remove our eyes from the wonderful sight.

Long after daylight, Rabbitskin was first to wake.

"How long have I been retired?" he asked, leaping up.

"Quite a while," Harry said. "You missed a beautiful night."

"I do apologize, good sirs. But I needed that."

Rabbitskin woke his companions while Yora and Tanjo crawled to their feet, stretched, and yawned. Ben and the Malones slowly opened their eyes simultaneously and rose together like robots.

Mr. and Mrs. Malone, who were once so outgoing and bubbly, had completely changed since our arrival on Rabistca. Ben had always been quiet and withdrawn, but not them. I liked them much better when they were acting. At least then, they were fun to be around and pretended to be happy.

The Carnavorines spent hours cleaning the campsite. The bony fish carcasses were returned to the river and the ashes from the fire were wiped clean and buried. They spared no detail. Harry and I chipped in and tried to make ourselves useful while the other Godlings, of course, did nothing.

When Rabbitskin was satisfied our campsite was in its original state, we continued on our way. Yora and Tanjo were once again placed on leashes and took their usual positions up front.

The Universal Forest was like a walk down memory lane. The Perigon Trail stretched wide and was easy to follow up and down the rolling hills of the Earth-like terrain. Huge pines lined the trail and covered our path with a thick carpet of pine needles. The fresh piney aroma was well-known to me, and every breath reminded me of home.

Although there were dangerous animals in the forest such as bears, wolves, tusk-dogs, and fox-cats, the threat was minimal. None would get anywhere near a Protector, and we walked fearlessly across the landscape.

After a few hours, the trail began to steadily rise until we found ourselves high on a smooth mountain range. Giant herds of elk, deer, and other unknown grazing animals could be seen crossing a vast grassy field below.

"Bald Rock surely has a wonderful view," Rabbitskin said, stopping to enjoy the scenery.

"It surely does," I agreed.

I took a few seconds to take it all in. I could see why this was the Carnavorines' most popular environment and was glad it was chosen for sections of Earth.

Rabbitskin was glowing. He had a smile on his face that could only be obtained by finally being home. For 600 years he'd done his duty well. I hated we were there to spoil the moment. He didn't seem to mind, though. The apeman was perfectly willing to share the spotlight. My fondness of him was growing by the minute. His heart was pure.

"We're close." Bowskin said, pointing ahead. "Sina lays there, deep beneath Mt. Skylar."

A snowcapped mountain loomed in the distance.

As I stared at Mt. Skylar, I began to feel nervous.

Everyone seemed to have a secret, and nobody was telling me the entire truth.

Chapter 18

After a brief stay at Bald Rock, we continued downward through the forest until we reached the open range I'd seen from the mountaintop. As soon we entered the grasslands, butterflies began to appear. At first there were hundreds, then thousands, and before long, millions. These charming little insects were all cut from the same mold. Each had bright, decorative, rainbow-colored wings attached to thin blue bodies.

As we made our way across the valley, I began see where the swarm was coming from. Our path was leading us to the most elegant garden I'd ever seen. Acres upon acres of gigantic flowers stood in perfect uniformed rows similar to a cornfield. Every stalk was bright blue with a single rainbow bloom on top, identically matching the butterflies hovering above them.

I suddenly stopped in my tracks.

Rainbow Roses and Rainbow Butterflies, I said to myself. This is Garden Valley. I know this place.

This wasn't like my previous visions, and it wasn't Deja vu. This was a place I'd physically been before, many times. It was my favorite place in the universe. I stared suspiciously at the garden for a long time trying to make sense of it all.

"Young Mr. Spencer. Mr. Spencer!" Rabbitskin finally said. "Is something wrong, sir?"

"I'm alright," I mumbled. "All these psychedelic butterflies must be making me dizzy or something. Let's keep going."

I wasn't dizzy. I'd just got my first glimpse of the Circle. I'd keep this to myself for now.

As soon as we took our first step inside the rose garden, butterflies began landing all over us. By the time we'd reached the center of the field, we were covered head to toe. Yora and Tanjo became unrecognizable and seemed embarrassed by their jazzy new look. It was all I could do not to burst out laughing. I don't know why I found this to be so amusing, but I did. Eventually we all morphed into walking rainbow silhouettes.

As we neared the end of the garden, the butterflies were stacked so high, it was difficult to walk. Thankfully, when we stepped past the last row of roses, all at the same time, the butterflies released us and flew back into their multicolored home.

"Do they do that every time?" Harry asked.

"Every single time," Rabbitskin said, smiling. "Mischievous little gents, but harmless nonetheless."

Garden Valley was behind us, but before we walked away, I took one good look back. Something here had triggered something deep inside me.

"Come on, sir," Rabbitskin told me, tugging at my shirt. "One more mountain to climb and I'll be home."

As we began the arduous climb up Mt. Skylar, there was no room for error. The Perigon Trail steeply narrowed and transformed into sharp, jagged rock. We again walked in single file. I bear-hugged the mountain, trying not to look down. The trail eventually led to an unmistakable set of rocky stairs. The steps were obviously shaped by bigger feet than mine. I clumsily tried to keep pace.

Yora and Tanjo scaled the stairs with little effort. The young cats glided up the steep incline, making a mockery of my continual struggle. Despite giving it my all, I began to lag behind.

"Hey!" I finally shouted, out of breath. "We all aren't 8-feet tall with size 24 feet."

Rabbitskin turned around and saw me floundering.

"Sorry, young lad," he said. "I guess I'm getting a little too anxious to see Sina."

I didn't blame Rabbitskin for wanting to get home. It just seemed that being the son of immortals, I should be able to fly or something. Didn't the title come with any privileges? Why should I have to hoof it everywhere? My feet were killing me. Anyway, despite all my bitching and moaning, we managed to gradually inch our way upward to the spot of the mountain where the snow began. I could now see the West River, the Canyon Wall, and Garden Valley in the distance. I couldn't believe how high we'd climbed.

As we slowly made our way toward the summit, the forest thinned, and eventually there was only one tree remaining on the snowy path — an ancient oak. Its roots had somehow bored through solid rock and had found a way to survive in the harshest conditions. Its snow-covered branches looked creepy, and although it appeared to be dead from its lack of greenery, the tree was very much alive.

"The Old Oak," Rabbitskin said, affectionally patting the massive, gray trunk. "Been here as long as anyone can remember. It's not that much to look at, but it does have one redeeming feature."

"What?" I said.

Rabbitskin methodically ran his hand across the tree as if he was searching for something. His brief hunt ended at a huge knot with a large gaping hole in the center. Rabbitskin placed his right arm deep into the opening and began to fish around.

"Ah huh," he finally said. "I knew you'd be there."

Rabbitskin stuck both arms into the hole and pulled out a small, dusty wooden barrel.

"What's that?" Harry asked.

"This, my friend, is Carnavorine whiskey. I put it here 600 years ago. It's been slowly aging since. A little homecoming present I made for myself."

Fellskin and Bowskin shrieked and whistled showing their approval. It even got Harry's attention who'd always loved his alcohol.

Rabbitskin sat down, resting his back against the old tree. He brushed the cobwebs off the whiskey container, grinned, and looked down at his prize.

"I knew the Old Oak would keep you from rotting," he said.

At the bottom of the barrel was a small cork. Protected by the power of the senior oak, it, too, had somehow survived through six long centuries.

Rabbitskin carefully pulled on the brown plug. The age-old stopper came out with little effort, making a muffled pop when it was released. A smooth, sweet aroma filled the air, placing us all into a mouth-watering stupor.

"Anyone want a sip?" Rabbitskin jokingly said.

"Ha ha," I replied.

I waited for the whiskey to come my way, and when it did, I wasn't disappointed. The smooth nectar ran down my throat like pure velvet. I closed my eyes and slowly swallowed trying to make it last as long as possible.

Everyone nestled against the Old Oak and passed the wooden barrel around. We all took part. No one was dumb enough to pass this up. We didn't budge until it was all gone.

"Thanks," I told Rabbitskin, after squeezing the last drop from the barrel. "Nothing could top that."

"Well, there's one thing that might," he said, bouncing up.

"What?"

"I left two barrels inside the tree."

Fellskin and Bowskin jumped up and began their tirade again. I was so happy I decided to join them, letting out a few whistles myself. Rabbitskin retrieved the other barrel, and we repeated the whole routine over again. I swear the second drum was even better than the first.

After we finished, we sat for a while and enjoyed the aftertaste, not to mention the buzz.

I was nervous about meeting the King.

Nothing like some liquid courage to help soothe the nerves.

Chapter 19

Sina. So many times I had visions of the city, but they were too brief, too blurry. Little did I know we were standing at the entryway.

When Rabbitskin led us to the back of the Old Oak, the backside was hollow.

"The Wooden Hole," Rabbitskin said, pointing to the opening. "The gateway to Sina."

Could this be the doorway to the most glorious city in the universe, I thought? My mind had painted a picture on a much grander scale. I figured there would be a band playing or two Carnavorines blowing into a conch shell or something.

I noticed a set of stairs leading downward.

One at a time, we filed down the steps, and were soon on solid ground. It was pitch black. I couldn't see a damn thing.

There was a commotion in the corner and the lights finally popped on. I couldn't believe it. We were standing in a fashionable, modern room. Talk about instant cultural shock. The floors and walls of the stylish chamber were shiny and reflected as mirrors. Unfortunately, our reflection was something I didn't necessarily need or want to see. I personally looked like I'd been to hell and back, even more gaunt than usual. Together, well, let's just say we were a motley crew, hairy and scary.

"Where are we?" I asked Rabbitskin, who was fiddling with some buttons on the far wall.

"Why young Mr. Spencer?" the apeman said. "Haven't you ever been inside an elevator?"

Before I had time to answer, Rabbitskin yelled, "Going down!" And we were off.

When we began our descent, the floors and walls that had first reflected our images transformed into an invisible glass. It was like we were hovering in space. I could feel the floor, but I couldn't see it. I walked forward with my arms extended until my hand hit the wall. It was there, all right. I wasn't hallucinating.

Yora and Tanjo seemed bored and cowered in the corner. This wasn't natural for them, and although they'd probably ridden the invisible elevator many times, I could tell they were unimpressed.

"Sina!" The word purred off Rabbitskin's tongue.

Sina was completely different than I'd imagined. It even got the undivided attention of The Four.

The city was still far below our position. It was hard to make out much detail from so high up, but it didn't appear to be nearly as large as an Earth city. Why should it be? The Carnavorine population numbered just over a thousand, and many were on assignment on other planets or the other two terrains. Regardless, what it lacked in size, it made up in stature.

There were thousands of bright glowing stalactites mounted to the ceiling and walls of the gigantic cave. They were everywhere. These luminous glassy structures looked like radiant ice sculptures, each having their own distinctive features. I was taken in by their splendor, and as we continued downward, I couldn't take my eyes off them. It felt like we were on the inside of the world's largest diamond.

"They're Sand Crystals," Rabbitskin told me, seeing my interest.

"I don't remember making these," Harry said, taking a closer look. "What planet are they found on?"

"They're not found on any planet, Sir Harry," Rabbitskin told him. "They're naturally manufactured on our most distant moon, Maloth. Each time the Supar rotates around our planet, it passes extremely close to Maloth. The small moon's surface is comprised mostly of a rare sand known as rask. When conditions are right, while passing Maloth, the Supar will send out a solar flare which strikes the moon with incredible force. When this powerful beam explodes into the rask, a Sand Crystal is formed. Their ability to store energy is like nothing we've ever encountered. They provide power to all of our underground cities. Sadly, harvesting the crystals is dangerous and comes at a great cost. Many Carnavorines have made the ultimate sacrifice collecting them."

I could tell this aggravated Harry. I don't think he appreciated the fact that there were compounds made from sources other than himself. I didn't want to spoil it for Rabbitskin, but I'd already figured this out. I shook my head, however, and looked surprised as though he was teaching me something new.

My attention quickly turned back to Sina which was getting closer by the second. We had probably already dropped 9,000 feet and were still only about halfway to the bottom.

I began to make out hundreds of rectangular structures along the cave floor. They were all similar in size and shape, each with a dim green glow.

High above all of the uniform structures were enormous tubes that encircled the city like bright wedding rings. I counted 11 tubes in all, each a thousand feet above the other. As they got higher, the rings became smaller conforming to the shrinking size of the mountain cavity. All of them were made from a golden shiny material that looked like polished brass. Only when we passed the first one did I realize how big they actually were.

"The Golden Bands of Sina," Rabbitskin said, glowing. "These are our personal housing units. The largest one on the bottom is where I reside, young Mr. Spencer."

"What are all those buildings on the cave floor?" I asked.

"That's the Green Houses!" Fellskin snapped. "You need not worry about them. It's forbidden to enter them without the King's written permission. You won't be allowed inside for any reason."

"Fellskin!" Rabbitskin cried out. "This isn't for you to decide. Apologize at once."

Fellskin told me he was sorry, but I could tell he didn't mean it. I didn't blame him. He had to be confused by our presence in his city. I needed to personally reassure him that I meant no harm.

"I promise I'll respect you and your traditions while inside your great city." I told the scorned apeman. "I want to thank you and your faithful Protectors for leading us safely to your humble home."

I kneeled onto the invisible floor at Fellskin's feet. Harry joined me.

This made Fellskin's facial expression totally change.

"Please forgive me, sir," Fellskin said. This time he meant it.

Rabbitskin was pleased with the exchange and gave me a nod of approval. Let's face it, I'd learned my gratitude from him. His unselfish ways were starting to wear off on me. I'd come a long way in a short amount of time. Even my swearing was getting better. Don't get me wrong, I could still drop the F Bomb at the drop of a hat, but for some reason I felt obligated to try and improve. I had to become more like Rabbitskin to gain respect among his leaders. Soon I would meet the King; better get it together.

As we passed the Golden Bands, each luminescent ring glittered across my face. The Sand Crystals were now high above, shining as a million stars. Even from a distance, their dazzle never dwindled.

I could now plainly see the Green Houses scattered along the cave floor. The Four were fixated on them. They gawked downward, ignoring everything else in the beautiful city. I thought this was rude and gave Harry a sharp nudge in the side.

When the elevator finally stopped, we came to rest parallel with the lowest, largest band. There was a faint smothered ring, and the invisible door slowly opened.

When we stepped out of the elevator, things that were invisible during our descent were now in full view.

There was a huge platform outside the door that encircled the elevator shaft. Hundreds of tiny walkways sprouted from the platform, all shooting to different parts of the Golden Band.

The unusual walkways were gravity defying. They seemed to be suspended in space. They had no railings. What kept them erect was anyone's guess. They looked liked spider webs and must've been woven from a super-strong compound that could easily support the heavy weight of the Carnavorines. Each individual strand was no bigger than a human hair, yet I marveled at how solid they felt underneath my feet.

The 10 Golden Bands above us had the same platforms and walkways. It didn't take me long to figure out what was going on. The platforms were needed to move around the city, but they destroyed the view. The elevator's glass acted as a two-way mirror. While inside the elevator, the walkways were rendered invisible. Since the Golden

Bands appeared to be made from a similar material, it probably worked the same while inside the ring-like housing units.

The glass must've worked in correlation with the material that the labyrinth of walkways was made from. What a wonderful technology. This product could've easily competed with the Maze-O's success back on Earth.

I told myself to ask Rabbitskin about this at a more appropriate time, for now, he seemed preoccupied.

Rabbitskin stood with his back to me, anxiously looking down one of the walkways. He wasn't moving a muscle. What was he doing?

Suddenly an opening formed in the Golden Band in front of him and a much smaller Carnavorine appeared in the doorway.

"Rainskin!" Rabbitskin shouted, taking off at a full sprint. Rainskin followed suit, and the two happy Carnavorines met in the middle of the walkway, locking into an unbreakable embrace.

"Who's that?" I whispered to Fellskin.

"Rainskin. Rabbitskin's life-mate."

It never dawned on me that Rabbitskin might have a significant other. Why hadn't he mentioned it? Imagine that, over 600 years apart. Well, at least she was with her people. Rabbitskin had been alone this whole time.

This made me realize why the Carnavorines wanted the Maze-O so badly. Their communication technology was their achilles heel. It could help them in many ways. Hell, if these two lovebirds would've had them during their years apart, they could've shared thoughts and even on-the-spot images of each other's journey.

I didn't know what male and female Carnavorines did behind closed doors, I wouldn't let that visual enter my mind, but we could always meet the King tomorrow. Tonight, Rabbitskin and Rainskin needed some alone time, and I was going to make sure they got it.

Rabbitskin walked back toward our position with Rainskin welded to his arm. He was a whole head taller than her, but besides that, they looked exactly alike.

Rainskin was introduced to me and The Four. She had a soft voice and was extremely polite. I could tell, though, she was thrown off by our presence.

I struck up some small talk using her native language. We chirped back and forth while Rabbitskin pulled Fellskin to the side for a private conversation.

I liked Rainskin. She reminded me of Rabbitskin. I wondered how the Carnavorines' relationships worked. It had to be complicated.

I was told that when one died, another was born. Males replaced males, and the same went for females, but did the females get pregnant, or did they just appear? When someone died, did the new Carnavorine replace the current mate? Did Carnavorines choose their mates or were they appointed by the King? Geez, I thought dating was tough back on Earth.

Soon Rabbitskin and Fellskin rejoined the group.

"You'll meet the King tomorrow," Fellskin informed us. "We could all use a good night's rest."

"And a bath," I added.

We'd been in the same clothes for days, and I couldn't wait to get cleaned up. It doesn't matter what planet you're from, smelling like ass is universal. Harry probably didn't mind. I'd never seen him in clean clothes.

"Fellskin will lead you to your quarters," Rabbitskin said. "Please forgive me for being rude, but I--"

"Just go and enjoy yourself, big guy." I snickered. "We'll probably survive the night without you."

I gave Rabbitskin a wink. He smiled back.

"Now go on," I said. "That's an order."

The newly reunited couple turned and pranced back down the walkway. They soon disappeared through the opening of the Golden Band. Once they were safely inside, the opening instantly turned solid again.

Bowskin grabbed Yora and Tanjo and got back into the elevator. I was hoping he was taking Yora to get more sophisticated medical attention. I was going to miss those two cats. I always felt safe with them around.

Fellskin led us down one of the many walkways to our room. Along the way, I could hear the Godlings secretly whispering behind me. I couldn't make out what they were saying, but I didn't need to.

I knew what they were mumbling about — the Green Houses.

Chapter 20

As we walked down the spiderweb walkway, I couldn't wait to see the housing units inside the Golden Bands. To tell the truth, I didn't know what to expect. Nothing could prepare me for what I was about to see, however. The Carnavorines' living quarters were modern, sleek, and hip. Dare I say feng shui.

The floors were made from one solid piece of wood, carved from an enormous tree. I knew this because of the countless tree rings that started in the middle of the floor and spiraled outward to the walls. Judging by the number of rings, the tree must've been a thousand years old. The old wooden floor was as hard as concrete, no doubt petrified. This made perfect sense. The Carnavorines wouldn't cut down a live tree.

Shockingly, the furniture was what might be found in an up-scale New York penthouse. There was a cozy faux suede couch, love seat, end tables, and coffee table in the middle of the living area. Beautiful sculptures, artwork and show pieces were flawlessly _arranged throughout the unit. The entire room was designed to perfection.

I loved the kitchen. The floor and countertops were solid Goya marble. The sink, refrigerator, and stove were all made from a shiny, thick blue glass. The Carnavorine condo had everything an Earth kitchen would have, except on a much larger and grander scale.

Fellskin gave us all a tour, and it got better with every room. He was a wonderful guide, taking time to explain each rare showpiece's origin and history.

There were two large bedrooms. The jumbo beds were built into the floors and made from premiere down, hand plucked from the belly of a roos.

As we methodically moved from room to room, dim mood lights automatically turned on and off. They were somehow activated by our position in the room. Every time I stopped to look at a picture, the frame would light up. As soon as I turned away, the light would turn off again. From every angle the lighting shifted and moved, keeping in perfect rhythm with our body movements.

I purposely lagged behind and scanned one of the bedrooms to make this happen over and over again. A little childish, I admit, but a serious cheap thrill.

Even my bathroom was a work of art. Why, I'd feel guilty taking a dump in such a lovely place. Lord knows I needed to. Those smoked trout had been rumbling around in my gut since we left the West River; damn strong swimmers, even after death.

When the tour was over, I gazed out of the now invisible glass of the Golden Band. What a view. As I had suspected, the walkways and platforms weren't visible from inside the living quarters. I noticed a few Carnavorines walking across them. It looked strange, like they were walking in midair. I edged closer to the magical metallic glass to make sure it was actually there. I could now see Sina in all her glory. I was speechless.

Only days ago, I thought Bigfoot was a nasty, mythical ape that scourged for food and lived on a dirty cave floor. From where I now stood, that notion was absurd. Matter of fact, nothing was further from the truth.

"I hope our accommodations will be sufficient," Fellskin said. "Two of you can stay here and the rest can follow me. There are plenty of rooms available. Many Carnavorines are on assignment and won't be back for years."

"Harry and I will take this one," I said, seizing the opportunity for some alone time with my father.

"Very well," Fellskin replied. "Make yourselves at home. The King will send for you tomorrow."

I thanked Fellskin and he left with Ben and the Malones following close behind. I wasn't going to miss those three. The tightlipped trio had been crude, boring, and mysteriously silent since our adventure had begun. Good riddance. Don't let the invisible door hit ya where the good lord split ya.

Harry was a different story. He'd showed promising signs during our travels, signs of true emotions and caring. I have to admit, other times, he simply seemed distant, cold, even confused.

It was time for Harry and I to finally clear the air. Let's just call it the big meeting before the big meeting. We'd had many private business meetings in the past, but this was going to be different. This time I was going to do the talking. You see, my power and knowledge had grown much greater than he'd anticipated. I knew everything, even The Four's dirty secrets.

Before I talked to Harry, though, I needed an hour or two to get cleaned up and decompress from the long trip. It seemed a lifetime ago since we arrived on Rabistca. The smell of my clothes might suggest two lifetimes.

I was told by Fellskin that the bath was voice-activated. I should've asked for more details. I stood in the bathroom, like an idiot, looking down at the marble tub wondering what to say to make it turn on. Honestly, I felt stupid.

"Tub on!" I shouted.

Nothing.

"Water?"

Nothing.

"H-2-0?"

Nothing.

It wouldn't have been so humiliating if I wasn't already naked. I must've looked ridiculous, the smartest guy in the universe talking to a damn tub.

Frustrated, I finally screamed out loud, "I just want a hot bath!"

Those must've been the magic words. Within a couple of seconds, the tub was full of hot sudsy water. There was no spigot. I couldn't figure out where it came from. This wasn't funny anymore. I was now getting out-smarted by an inanimate object.

My frustration was brief. The steam from the hot bath was calling my name. I eased down into the large tub. Ahh! The temperature was perfect. I melted in.

You know, I was proud of the things I'd invented in my lifetime, but the person who invented the tub, now there was a real genius. Maybe the greatest invention of all time, save the wheel.

After a few minutes of basking in the bubbles, I had a wild thought. It probably wouldn't work, but what the hell.

"Music!" I commanded.

It didn't surprise me that music began to play, but what surprised me was the song — Yellow Submarine by the Beatles. I guess, even on Rabistca, a classic is a classic. I leaned back and let the soothing voice of legendary singer Ringo Star take me to dreamland.

I stayed in the tub for hours listening to the classics. I requested one after another and they all played without skipping a beat. I really needed this. Tomorrow, all eyes would be on me, but for now, I was just an ordinary nerd splashing around in a bubble bath without a care in the world.

After a few hours in the Carnavorine tub, I was shriveled up like a prune. I didn't want to leave. Eventually, though, I forced myself out of the soothing water. When I finally did, I took my clothes and threw them into my bath water. They stunk to high heaven and needed a good soaking. Unfortunately, this left me in a bind. I was soaking wet and butt naked with nothing to wear. I didn't look in the mirror. Seeing myself without clothing was something I always tried to avoid. My reflection only reminded me once again why I was still a virgin. I wasn't exactly model material.

There had to be a towel or something I could temporarily wrap myself with. I scanned the room for closets. There were none.

"Wi wiup wii wi wup we," I commanded. Translation: Bath towel, please.

To my surprise, a door appeared on the far wall. Hanging in the closet were four extra-large white robes. Each was embroidered with the name Deerskin on the upper right side. On a shelf next to them were some huge, fluffy matching towels, perfectly folded and neatly stacked.

"Thank youuu, Mr. Deerskin!" I said out loud.

I toweled myself off and slipped into one of Deerskin's robes. The sleeves dangled past my arms and the robe dragged the ground well below my feet. This gigantic robe was obviously not made for shrimps, but it was soft, clean, and warm; even smelled nice.

I rolled the sleeves up and clumsily stumbled out into the living room. Of course, there stood Harry, with the exact same over-sized garment. He was standing with his back to me, looking out at the underground city.

"I've been watching the Carnavorines for an eternity," Harry said without turning around. "But this is the first time my eyes have seen the grandeur of the Golden Bands."

"Cut the shit, Harry," I snapped. "You've seen the Golden Bands plenty of times. Just not as an invited guest."

Harry twisted around and glared at me.

"You've come too far, too fast!" he scolded, aiming his boney finger at me. "Who are you to judge me? Your short life has been a mere fraction of a second. Only one quick breath. You know nothing of The Four's struggles. Some things take time, Logan Some things you have to live through to understand."

I immediately struck back. I wasn't about to be bullied into this kind of conversation. This was going to go in the direction that I dictated.

"What does a person who's lived 26 years and a person who's lived forever have in common?" I asked.

My riddle seemed to intrigue Harry. He thought for a minute but couldn't retrieve the answer from his monstrosity of a brain.

My father then said three simple words I thought I'd never hear from Harry Fox — "I don't know."

Once I recovered from the shock, I gave him the answer.

"They both have to live with themselves," I told him.

You see, Harry was at the crossroads. It's the classic good vs. evil, right vs. wrong. His plan had been specific all these years, but that changed when I came along. He tried to fight it. Hell, he was still trying fighting it, but there is no fighting unconditional love. My mom didn't have it, but he did, yet he didn't understand it any more than he understood the Carnavorines.

I was tired of pussyfooting around, tired of these stupid mind games and mirror tricks. It was time to lay it on the line.

"You didn't father me out of love," I told Harry. "You fathered me out of need. I was nothing more than a science project used to get

105

you closer to your final objective. Tell the truth, father, The Four are here to destroy the Carnavorines!"

"Lower your voice," Harry whispered, peeping around. "Please, let's have a seat in the living room and talk. Talk like we used to back on Maze Island. Let's sit together, my son, and I'll tell you everything."

We walked over and sat on the couch facing the city. Harry looked unsettled.

It was time for the lies to end and he knew it. Harry was perfectly aware of my capabilities. There was no hiding from me now. Nothing could slip past my X-ray vision, past, present or future.

"Logan," he whispered.

Harry looked up at me like a lost puppy. He didn't know where to begin. It didn't matter. It was my time for me to become the teacher, my time to set things straight.

"I know that The Four are here to steal the Carnavorines' secrets," I revealed. "But why? Isn't it enough that you control the planets, stars, and moons? I know your desires; I feel your jealousy. But you don't need to feel this way. How can you not see it, when it's right in front of your face? You did it, Harry! Don't you get it? You've already accomplished what you seek."

"What are you talking about Logan?" Harry cried out. "I've tried for a trillion years. I simply cannot create life!"

I placed my hand on my father's knee. "You already have, Harry. You created me."

There was a long, uncomfortable pause, and it finally happened. It wasn't rehearsed. It wasn't practiced. Harry Fox began to cry, and it was beautiful.

This was the moment I'd been waiting for. I wasn't sure it was going to happen, but it finally did. I needed Harry. Without him, even I was no match against The Four.

Now it was three against three, much better odds. Me, Harry and Rabbitskin, were in one corner. Ben, Mr. and Mrs. Malone in the other.

You see, I knew something that I hadn't told anyone. There was going to be war, the greatest battle the universe had ever seen. This conflict wouldn't be fought with advanced weaponry or well-trained armies of men. Instead, it would be fought with the mind, and more important, the heart.

Harry started telling me everything. I already knew what he had to say, but I listened anyway; not for me. I listened for him. He needed to come clean, confess his sins. Besides, that's what people with true emotions do, something he needed to learn.

Harry was no longer a cold, robotic scientist. He'd become a God with a conscience. This happened because now he had something to lose, something that was much more important than his undying lust for the Carnavorines formulas. That something was, me.

While Harry was confessing, real emotions began to pour out. He went through them all. It was great watching him deal with each new one; sorrow, regret, anger, worry, joy, love, compassion. Watching him experience emotions for the first time was religious.

Everything changed that day. Harry kept his promise. He told me everything. By the time he'd finished, he was reborn.

Harry Fox was no longer on the fence.

Chapter 21

Before we continue, it's important for you to know what Harry told me that day. It's about time you knew what I was up against.

You must understand, most of what Harry had already told me was true. The Four were scientists. Harry did discover the Power of Zero. I was Harry's son. My father did create this universe as well as many others. The Fours' struggle to find the Carnavorine's secrets and their desire to find their maker were all true.

However, he did leave out a few important details.

The Four couldn't figure out how to create life. This drove them absolutely mad. They didn't understand how they could create worlds but couldn't grow a single-cell organism. Long before I was in the picture, the Godlings began to resent the Carnavorines, hate them. Despise the very thought of them.

When the Carnavorines built the Halls of Goya, that was the last straw. Rock was their turf. Out of jealousy, Harry placed the Silver Stone to block the entrance. The gloves were off.

From that point on, the Godlings decided to get the Carnavorines' secrets by any means necessary. In short, they decided to steal them.

This wasn't Harry's first trip to Rabistca; far from it. Matter of fact, The Four knew the planet like the back of their hands. They spent most of their time studying and following the Carnavorines' routines.

Through years of careful planning, they finally managed to sneak into one of the Green Houses, but it didn't help. They had no idea what they were looking at. They even stole samples and studied them back on Maze Island; still didn't help. This made them angrier.

At some point, they even discussed destroying this universe, but that would only leave them alone again. They were stuck and consumed by jealousy. That's why envy was their only real emotion. They lived and breathed it.

Hopeless and disgruntled, Harry went back to the drawing board. That's when he had an idea. They'd try to produce a child; not to love, but to study.

They didn't know how I'd turn out, so they watched closely. It didn't take them long to realize I was special. I was learning at a worrisome rate. It dawned on them early on that I might become smart enough to learn the Carnavorines' secrets, but they had to be sure.

The Maze-O was Harry's grand scheme, and it worked perfectly on all fronts. It tested my skills while simultaneously grabbing the attention of the Carnavorines.

Through me, they assumed the Carnavorines' secrets would be easily obtainable. Once they had the formulas, they'd destroy this universe, wipe away all traces of their failures here. Afterwards, they'd create their own lifeforms in an alternate world, and make them way better than those pesky Carnavorines.

Along the way, however, Harry got to know me. He liked me, eventually loved me. He tried to fight it, but he couldn't. He even moved to the Getaway Ranch to get away from me. Ben had told the Malones that Harry was getting too close. They thought separating us might solve the problem, but Harry's fondness only grew stronger.

As for The Three, during our journey across Rabistca, they were being silent for good reason. They were pissed off. They saw how much I liked Rabbitskin and it infuriated them. They simply couldn't understand why we were becoming friends. I was a traitor in their eyes, but not Harry's. He liked Rabbitskin, too, and his internal conflict became even more torn.

Make no mistake about it, this was The Four's last-ditch effort to get their way.

Their back up plan was straightforward; if I couldn't give them what they wanted, this universe was to be destroyed. Matter of fact, even if I could deliver the goods, they had no intentions of taking me with them. They still didn't know if I was immortal, but if possible, I was to be eliminated. They'd simply chalk me up as an experiment gone wrong.

This was my dilemma. With or without the Carnavorines' secrets, The Four intended to wipe this universe off the face of the map.

Now you see what I was up against.

That's why I needed Harry — to save myself, your sorry asses, and the Carnavorines.

Chapter 22

Harry had finally come full circle. He was no longer a cardholding member of The Four. Unbeknownst to them, they'd just become The Three.

Harry and I understood the severity of our problem. The Three were powerful, smart, and bitter; a lethal combination. They weren't going to be persuaded; they'd have to be defeated. This wasn't going to be easy. Luckily, we had one thing going for us, something that might give us a slight advantage — the element of surprise.

While Harry was still recovering from his emotional breakdown, I racked my brain trying to figure out the best way to proceed. My visions had showed me the truth, but only in pieces and parts. I needed more time to put it all together.

I had to somehow return to Garden Valley. That's where I'd find the answer. That's where I got my first glimpse of the Circle. I couldn't put my finger on it, but that place had special meaning.

What I really needed was a diversion, something that would allow me to secretly sneak back to the valley without raising too much suspicion.

We had to keep The Three believing they could still get their hands on the Carnavorines' secrets. I needed something to keep them occupied, something to hold their attention for a day or so. That would give me more time to learn about the Circle. The big meeting would have to be pushed back until I could complete my journey.

I had a plan, but if it was going to work, Harry, the Carnavorines, and I would have to work together. Each would have to play their parts perfectly. It was time for us to become a unified team, an honest team. No more games, secrets, or lies; it was our only chance.

Somehow, I had to let the Carnavorines know what was going on. Without their full support, we couldn't pull this off. This is the part that frightened me most. My plan might require them to break one of their Sacred Laws, but it was the only way. Their very lives depended on it.

I knew what had to be done.

"Harry, where are those Maze-Os we removed at your cabin?" I asked.

"I still have them,' he said

"Great."

I hated to do it, but we had to find Rabbitskin. I hoped he had plenty of time to fulfill his apely duties.

Harry and I threw on our wet clothes and snuck out onto the walkway. We could only pray that The Three weren't watching. We darted back to the main platform where the elevator was located. I looked at all the walkways trying to remember which one Rainskin had walked down earlier.

"This is it," Harry told me.

"You sure?"

"You're kidding, right?" Harry said, smiling.

"What was I thinking?"

We ran down the walkway toward Rabbitskin's living quarters.

When we got close to the Golden Band, the door opened, and we cautiously walked inside. To my surprise, we were standing in a room full of Carnavorines.

I instantly recognized Babbleskin. He was covered in thick, gray fur. The other Carnavorines had to be the Council of Ten. Rainskin was nowhere to be found.

I couldn't have planned this any better myself, the 11 individuals I needed to talk to, all in the same room.

They didn't share my enthusiasm.

The Carnavorines had known something was wrong. Rainskin was merely a ploy to get the Council together for a secret meeting. The Four never gave enough credit to the Carnavorines. They were courteous as hell, but shrewd to the bone. Pulling the wool over their eyes was almost impossible. Like me, Rabbitskin was also suspicious of the Godlings. He had personally called this private gathering.

Before anyone had time to say anything, I kneeled on the floor at Babbleskin's feet. Harry followed suit.

"We humbly seek your counsel," I told the King. "If you'll allow me, I'll reveal the truth and put your minds at rest. Harry and I are friends of the Carnavorines. But I need to speak without interruption. Time is not on our side, and all of our lives are at stake."

Rabbitskin smiled down at me. He was impressed with my perfect manners and newfound statesmanship. I wasn't the cocky, filthy-mouthed degenerate he had chastised just days earlier. I could tell by his expressions that he was proud of me — Mr. Professionalism.

"Is this the one?" the King asked Rabbitskin, in a deep voice.

"Yes sir. This is Logan Spencer, and I believe we can trust him."

"Please speak, my son," Babbleskin said. "But speak with your heart. We know your mind is great, but the heart never lies. Take your time and start from the beginning."

For hours, I poured my heart out. I told them everything. They heard the exact same story I'm currently broadcasting to you. I even told them of my visions and why I must go back to Garden Valley. I left absolutely nothing out.

When I was finished, it was Harry's turn. Although it shamed him, he told of his years of hatred and jealousy toward the Carnavorines. He went into great detail about his deceptions and lies. It couldn't have been easy.

The Carnavorines were on the edge of their seats as Harry told the story of the Silver Stone, and why he had blocked the entrance. He spoke of their ancestors, referring to them by name. He spoke of their history. He knew more about them than they knew about themselves. By the time he'd finished, his audience was at a loss for words, but thoroughly convinced of his authenticity.

Babbleskin nodded in approval. He knew we spoke the truth.

"Can we defeat The Three?" the King plainly asked me.

"I have a plan," I said. "But as King, you'll have to make some tough decisions."

I asked Rabbitskin to introduce us to the Council. The fate of the universe was in their hands. A formal introduction was in order.

Rabbitskin walked us around the room.

From the desert — there was Snakeskin, Sandskin, and Sunskin.

From the ocean — Fishskin, Frogskin, and Moonskin.

From the forest — Woodskin, Treeskin, and Lambskin.

Rabbitskin was the overseer of all three terrains, and second in command of the Carnavorines, sort of like Vice President, and next to be King. I had no idea he was so high in rank. Now I understood why Fellskin and Bowskin held him in such high regard. He was royalty.

With the introductions behind us, it was time to put my scheme into action.

We had a formidable team and a solid plan.

I hoped it would be enough.

Chapter 23

Asking the Carnavorines to break one of their Sacred Laws wasn't going to be easy. They weren't called the Wishy-Washy Laws. They were called the "Sacred" Laws, and that's why I was having trouble saying what needed to be said.

"What you ask is difficult, but not impossible," the King surprisingly said. "To enter a Green House only requires written permission by the King. I choose who enters. Does that put your mind at ease, Mr. Spencer?"

The Godlings weren't the only ones who'd underestimated the Carnavorines. So had I. It wouldn't happen again.

"Please tell us your plan," Babbleskin said. "I can assure you the Carnavorines will do our part."

My plan was simple. I had to get back to Garden Valley and complete my knowledge of the Circle. I was hoping it wouldn't take long, but I had no real way of knowing. That's why our diversion had to be rock solid. The Three had to be so preoccupied they'd forget all about me.

Babbleskin had already figured out my diversionary tactic.

As King, he'd invite The Three on a long, private tour of the Green Houses. They had dreamed about this for ages and would eagerly agree. Sure, they'd snuck in a few times, but a personal tour as VIPs? It'd be a no brainer.

So not to raise too many eyebrows, Harry would have to go along. It wouldn't be very difficult for him. He was damn good at role-playing. However, we did need to communicate. That's why we needed the Maze-Os.

Six Maze-Os had been removed back at Harry's cabin, one from each of The Three, two from Harry, and one from me. Babbleskin, Rabbitskin, Harry, and I would all have one installed. I gave Harry back his two. I still didn't ask. Good communication would be crucial if we were going to pull this off.

The one remaining Maze-O would go to Snakeskin, who could pass along information to the rest of the Council.

From basic materials found in Rabbitskin's apartment, Harry rigged up a device to attach all the Maze-Os. I used some common kitchen utensils to make some minor adjustments, and soon all six Maze-Os were securely attached and operational.

The three Carnavorines loved this new technology. Watching their reactions reminded me of the first time I experienced it. I gave the apemen a quick crash course in communications. They were fast learners and had no problem absorbing the information.

Once everyone felt comfortable, I wanted to go over my plan. I needed to make sure everyone was on the same page. We only had one shot at this.

I gathered everyone in the room for final instructions.

First the King, along with three members of the Council, would go to The Three's room and tell them some wonderful news. Babbleskin was going to accompany them on a private tour of the Green Houses.

Lambskin, Moonskin, and Sunskin would also be present as representatives of all three environments. Desert, Ocean, and Forest would all be in attendance to make the tour seem more official. The Three would be informed that the tour was going to be extensive. Basically, they'd be shown the entire operation from beginning to end. The King would offer this as a gesture of goodwill before the big meeting.

"Lay it on thick," I insisted.

I strongly suggested that the King make a heartfelt speech about working as a team, and how the two races must work together for the good of the universe. They'll eat it up. Make no mistake about it, though, working together will be the last thing on their minds.

"Once they've agreed," I instructed the King, "have The Three follow your entourage to our room. Then make Harry and I the same offer. Harry will eagerly agree, but I'll politely decline."

"That'll make them suspicious," Harry said.

"It'll make them a bit nervous," I agreed. "So, I'll privately tell them something that'll help calm their nerves."

"What?" Babbleskin said.

"I'm going to tell them the truth."

"Not a good idea," Harry told me.

"Why would you do this?" Rabbitskin questioned.

"Hold on," Babbleskin said.

Babbleskin paused and took a good long look at me. The King grinned and slightly nodded.

"Brilliant, young Mr. Spencer. Brilliant. Please continue."

"There's a saying back on Earth," I said. "The truth will set you free. Well, in this case, the truth will set me free. I'll tell The Three exactly what I plan to do."

Most everyone in the room still looked confused. I guess I needed to stop with the corny anecdotes and get directly to the point.

"I'm close to knowing the Carnavorines secrets," I'll tell them. "But I need time to piece my visions together. Then, I'll simply tell them the same thing I told you."

"I still don't follow," Snakeskin said, shaking his head.

"I'm gonna tell The Three that they're the diversion," I told the apeman. "I'll ask them to keep you in the Green Houses as long as possible. Stretch out the tour, I'll say. Give me the precious time I need to return to Garden Valley."

"Damn, it is brilliant," Harry agreed.

"With Harry playing along," I said, "they won't suspect a thing. They'll think they're the diversion, not the King."

At this point, I had everyone's undivided attention. Before my very eyes, and to my surprise, I was becoming a leader. The fate of the universe was on my shoulders and everyone knew it. They were beginning to believe in me. I sensed it. I was no longer that snotty-nosed kid that Harry rudely interrupted 10 years ago. I was ready to take the reins.

"What will you need for your journey?" Babbleskin asked.

"With your permission, I request that Rabbitskin travel with me. Whatever happens out there, I want someone near I can trust, and who knows the lay of the land."

Rabbitskin gave me a subtle nod. He was as fond of me as I was of him. I definitely wanted him around in case something unexpected happened, but more than anything, I wanted him with me as a friend.

"Anything else?" the King asked.

"I'd hope that Yora and Tanjo could be our assigned Protectors, if they're okay to travel on such short rest."

"Yora and Tanjo are always ready to fulfill their duties," the King proclaimed. "Two of our finest young Protectors. I'll have Fellskin and Bowskin prepare the cats and have them waiting at the Old Oak. They'll be ready when you arrive."

"What should I do?" Snakeskin asked. "I haven't been assigned a task. Why did I receive a Maze-O?"

"You and the rest of the Council, who are not a part of the Green House tour, return to the Halls of Goya and prepare for the big meeting," I said. "Through our Maze-Os, I'll keep you and everyone updated on my progress. There are still many unanswered questions here. Be ready for anything."

My plan was finalized, and the stage was set. It was time for us to split up and carry out our individual assignments.

Snakeskin would return to the Halls of Goya with the five unassigned Carnavorines.

Harry, Babbleskin, and three members of the Council had a long, fake tour to give.

Rabbitskin and I had a date with Garden Valley.

Chapter 24

The Three followed my secret script word for word. Their incessant greed made them predictable. Once they found out they were going to the Green Houses, they couldn't see past their own noses. It was like shooting fish in a barrel.

When Babbleskin came to our room, The Three were already following him around like eager children. The Godlings barely blinked when I pulled them aside and explained my plan. The Green Houses were a perfect shield. They didn't suspect a thing. The King's entourage scooped-up Harry and went on their way.

Once the coast was clear, I used my Maze-O to alert Rabbitskin. Within minutes, he arrived ready to travel. I was happy to reunite with my good friend. Just seeing his big, goofy mug made me smile.

"So, young Mr. Spencer," Rabbitskin said, placing his hands on my shoulders. "It appears you might become a gentleman yet, good sir."

"Don't speak too fast," I told him. "I've still got plenty of piss and vinegar left in me."

"I see that you do," he replied. "But your lack of manners has been offset by your honor. The Carnavorines owe you a great debt, young lad."

"But I haven't done anything yet," I said.

"Oh, but you have, good sir. You've chosen right over wrong. That's not always easy to do."

Rabbitskin always had a eloquent way of putting things into proper perspective. I didn't know what I'd face in Garden Valley, but whatever it was, it'd be less stressful with him tagging along.

I don't know why, but Rabbitskin's approval was important to me. It's ironic; somehow an ape had helped me become a man. It wasn't one thing in specific. Maybe it was his tender way of leading by example. He was proud of me, and that made me proud of myself. We were fast becoming best friends.

Rabbitskin and I scooted across the platform and hopped into the elevator. As we started our ascent, I stared down at the splendor of Sina. The stakes couldn't be any higher. This had to work.

When we reached the top of the elevator shaft, I ran up the stairs and shot through the Wooden Hole. It felt good to be back in the open. Sina was great, but I was no cave dweller.

I turned around to check on Rabbitskin and was greeted with two, big wet tongues across the face. It was Yora and Tanjo.

"Hey there, you two!" I said, engaging in a game of play wrestling. I'd grown fond of the cats, and it looked like the feeling was mutual. Fellskin and Bowskin were standing by the Old Oak enjoying the show. Rabbitskin was close by, laughing.

I was still puzzled by the cats' candid affection toward me. The Protectors' instinct was to serve the Carnavorines, not me. Why was I the exception?

Fellskin gave Rabbitskin a large pouch of water from the West River. Bowskin handed him a smaller satchel stuffed with roos jerky.

"Hopefully we won't be longer than a day, maybe two," Rabbitskin told his kinsmen.

"Sir," Fellskin said. "Bowskin and I know something's wrong. Whatever you're facing, we'll gladly face it with you. Please, we offer our very lives."

I walked over to Fellskin.

"You serve your people well," I told him.

"You'll have to wait here," Rabbitskin intervened. "Take comfort in the fact that we have powerful and trustworthy allies in our endeavors. Sorry I can't tell you more."

Fellskin had spoken his piece. Although he wanted to go with us, he respected the chain of command.

We said our goodbyes and went on our way.

Yora and Tanjo vaulted in front and began sniffing the trail ahead. Their restraints were no longer needed. They'd proven themselves during the slyth attack.

Once again, I found myself on the steep, jagged steps of Mt. Skylar. It was no easier going down than coming up. Actually, it was much scarier. Probably because I was forced to look downward, which only reminded me how high we were.

I began nervously hugging the mountain wall again, clawing my way down one step at a time. I was moving at a snail's pace. After watching this painful ritual for a while, Rabbitskin couldn't contain himself any longer.

"Should I give you a piggyback ride, young lad?" He said. "My life expectancy is only 1,200 years, and I fear I won't be alive by the time we reach the bottom."

"Very funny," I replied. "Just what I need right now. Bigfoot the comedian."

I knew that would probably ruffle his fur. He hated the name Bigfoot.

Without saying another word, Rabbitskin yanked me up, heaved me onto his back, and began storming down the mountain. I locked my arms around his neck and shoulders and held on. Downward we charged, while I bounced up and down uncontrollably on the apeman's back. For a large fellow, Rabbitskin could run like the wind. One by one, the rocky steps were tamed by his gigantic stride.

Yora and Tanjo easily kept pace, staying just ahead of us. Our new-and-improved speed was more suitable to their abilities. Let's face it, I was the asshole slowing everyone down.

Imagine how I felt; the son of an immortal on a quest to save the universe, having to be carried down the mountain like an infant. As humiliating as it was, though, I have to admit, it was productive. We reached Garden Valley in no time.

When the piggyback ride was over, Rabbitskin had to practically peel me off his shoulders. He offered an apology, but I wasn't mad. We didn't have time for my inefficient crawling technique. To be honest, the visual of us pounding down that mountain still cracks me up. It just wasn't so funny at the time.

Once the dust had settled, I looked across Garden Valley. The Rainbow Roses and Rainbow Butterflies were on full display. I scanned the horizon for any signs or visions; nothing yet. Hopefully something would happen soon. It had to, or we were in big trouble.

Rabbitskin stood behind me waiting for my next move, but I was unable to take another step. I seemed to be stuck.

I turned to my friend.

"I'm afraid," I whispered.

I began to weep.

A week ago I was sitting behind a desk at Preotec, minding my own business. Now, the fate of the universe was on my shoulders. I was crushed by fear, paralyzed by the unknown.

Rabbitskin placed his hand softly on the back of my head, and pulled me in. I guess everyone needs a hug sometimes. Yora and Tanjo joined in. Each took an ear and began licking.

Rabbitskin's warmth filled me with courage, and the Protectors' love gave me strength. I took a deep breath and tried to compose myself. Now wasn't the time for this mushy nonsense. We could ill-afford a chicken-hearted meltdown on my behalf.

"I have to go alone," I told Rabbitskin, pointing at the garden.

"I know you do, sir," he said. "But I can assure you, nothing short of death will remove me from this spot. I'll be here when you return. Do what you must, young lad."

I turned and faced Garden Valley.

Millions of butterflies hovered above the roses, waiting for a new playmate to cross their path. They were always on the lookout for a willing participant to play their favorite game.

I slowly walked forward and let them overtake me. They came in droves. Waves of butterflies began piling on me at an alarming rate. They were much more aggressive than before, and it didn't take long for them to stack hundreds of feet into the air.

Dark clouds formed overhead, and the wind kicked up. The insects began flying in a tight circular pattern that shortly turned into a a spiraling funnel cloud. The swirling mass flew faster and faster and started spinning out of control. The wind was blowing so hard that Rabbitskin had to drop to his knees. Yora and Tanjo dug their claws into the ground, to keep from blowing away. Suddenly, there was this violent swooshing sound, and the entire swarm was sucked into the heavens.

Rabbitskin ran over to where I'd been standing. There was no sign of me. He walked through the garden, searching for clues, but it was useless. Whatever had taken the butterflies, had also taken me.

Not only had I vanished, but so had every butterfly in the valley. The once-thriving community was now a ghost town. This had an immediate effect on the Rainbow Roses. Without their colorful counterparts, they began to weaken, wither, and lean. Seconds later, the roses fell.

Yora and Tanjo walked over to Rabbitskin, and loudly whimpered. As Protecters, they thought they'd failed. For now, there was nothing Rabbitskin could do. As promised, he wouldn't budge until I returned.

Chapter 25

Everything was moving in slow motion. The butterflies appeared to be flapping their wings at one frame per second. When I reached out my arms, the attached insects left lengthy traces of light behind them. I waved my hands in a circular pattern, which caused a drawn-out starburst effect. I quickly realized I was inside a cosmic ray.

How could this be, I thought? A cosmic ray was my untested theory. What was causing this phenomenon?

By my calculations, it would only take seconds to travel through a cosmic ray. From my distorted viewpoint inside the ray itself, it felt much longer. I playfully poked at a few slow-motion butterflies, but my entertainment was short-lived. Everything started speeding up. The ride was coming to an end. When we finally stopped, to my surprise, I was still standing at the edge of Garden Valley.

The butterflies promptly let go and flew back to the field.

Rabbitskin was nowhere to be found. I knew he'd never leave me. Something was wrong. I tried to use my Maze-O, but it didn't work.

Nearby, something began stirring inside the rose garden. The butterflies were gathering in that direction, which could only mean one thing. They were accumulating on a warm body.

I focused on the commotion and tried to stay calm. It wasn't easy. The mass was now heading straight for me. Closer and closer the butterflies came until I could hear heavy, crunching footsteps beneath them.

The swarm punched through the Rainbow Roses, coming to rest directly in front of me. I stood terrified as the butterflies unattached themselves and whisked back into the garden.

My jaw dropped. I was standing face to face with myself.

"Are you okay?" the Other Me said.

"Not really," I replied.

"Not really," he said, at the same time.

The Other Me must've known what I was going to say. I decided to test him further. I began thinking of a number.

"Twelve billion, two hundred forty-seven million, three hundred eighty-four thousand, nine hundred sixty-seven and one third," he answered, precisely as I was thinking it.

"This isn't funny." I told him. "Is there a point to this?"

"Come on," the Other Me said, chuckling. "Let's go sit under that tree. You have questions, so let's get comfortable."

I followed myself over to a humongous Redwood. This tree wasn't in Garden Valley. I obviously wasn't on Rabistca anymore.

"Going forward, you must trust me," the Other Me said, squatting onto the ground. "I'm here to help. Besides, if you can't trust yourself, who can you trust?"

I didn't know where to start. Picking my brain had to be handled with care. I might tell myself something I didn't want to hear.

"Where are we?" I asked. "This isn't Rabistca."

"This is your future home," he revealed. "In time, you'll possess the power to create worlds like Harry, only better. Planet Logan is a blend of all your favorite places in the universe. This is an upgraded version of Garden Valley, which has always been dear to our hearts."

"Our hearts?" I said. "Are we not two different people?"

"Don't you already know?" the Other Me said. "I'm you, in the future. We're the same."

"How's that possible?" I asked.

"You'll learn many things in coming times," he explained. "You only think you're smart now, Logan. Your mind will lead you to places you can't imagine."

I hated to be rude, but I didn't have time for this futuristic bullshit. I had more pressing issues that demanded my immediate attention; for starters, the Circle.

"Ahh, the Circle," the Other Me said. "Now we're finally getting somewhere."

"Will you stop doing that!" I told myself. "It's freaking me out!"

The Other Me wasn't flustered at all. He was calm, polite, and easygoing, reminded me of Rabbitskin. I was glad I'd eventually learn to control my emotions, but for now, I didn't like this Other Me. He probably didn't even swear or drink whiskey. Was this my future, a riddle-telling, smart ass?

"Just tell me what I need to know," I finally said. "Asking you anything is redundant."

The Other Me laughed. I think he was enjoying seeing himself, you know, the way he used to be. I guess one day I'll be sitting where he is, and this will be much more enjoyable.

Wait a minute, I thought. That's the Circle!

The Other Me was letting me figure out things for myself. Why wouldn't he? That's what I'd do. All of a sudden, a crazy thought popped into my head. I tried to shake it off, but I couldn't.

"That's it," the Other Me said. "Don't be frightened. Tell me what you're thinking. Tell me what you already know."

I did know. Deep down, I'd known for a while.

"I'm the creator," I reluctantly said.

"Go on," the Other Me replied.

"I created the Carnavorines and The Four," I mumbled.

My heart began racing out of control.

"Calm down," the Other Me said. "Take a minute and think logically. Push aside your emotions."

I sat in silence thinking about the Circle. How many times had it run its course? At least once, the Other Me was proof of that. Could it be hundreds?

"The Circle is infinite," the Other Me said. "But the future isn't set in stone. If The Three aren't stopped, all is lost."

"Can you help me?" I asked.

"NO! It'd tear a rift in the Circle," the Other Me warned. "I can't tell you what to do; you must figure that out yourself."

The Other Me had a valid point. If I knew what was coming, I wouldn't react instinctively. I'd overanalyze my next move, and screw everything up.

I wasn't told much that day, but I did learn one thing. The Four wouldn't live forever. At some point, they'd die, and when the Circle came back around, I'd have to create them again. Without Harry, I couldn't be born. Without me, neither could he.

Thinking about the Circle was mind-blowing. Thinking about it too much would result in a migraine.

Suddenly, a familiar voice called out from the Rainbow Roses.

"Hurry, young lad, the trout are practically jumping onto the bank."

"Is that Rabbitskin?" I said.

Without warning, the Rainbow Butterflies gobbled me up and we took off again.

I'll never forget what the Other Me said as I was leaving.

"Good luck, Logan," he yelled. "If you succeed, the next time we meet, I'll be you, and you'll be me."

I could hear him laughing as I was being swept away.

Chapter 26

Back on Rabistca, there was a massive explosion in the sky. The blast ruptured the clouds, and butterflies began pouring down from the heavens like rain. The Rainbow Roses suddenly sprang to life, once again returning Garden Valley to full bloom.

Yora and Tanjo lunged in front of Rabbitskin. They wouldn't let this phenomenon claim another victim; not on their watch.

The colorful swarm coasted downward with me in tow. When my feet were planted firmly on the ground, they hightailed it back to their real garden home.

Rabbitskin ran to my side.

"Young Mr. Spencer are you alright?" he shouted.

"How long have I been gone?" I asked.

"Three hours, maybe four."

"That's a relief," I said.

Now I had to make a decision. Should I tell Rabbitskin about my trip to the future? I wasn't sure how he'd take it. I was having a hard time with it myself.

In the end, I decided to tell him everything. Besides, the Other Me obviously wanted me to. He made sure I heard Rabbitskin's voice. He wasn't supposed to help, but he dropped a clever hint. That sounded more like me.

"Can we go to the West River?" I asked Rabbitskin "We need to talk."

"Of course, sir."

I didn't know why, but out of respect, I wanted to tell Rabbitskin somewhere he felt at ease.

Not much was said during our lengthy walk through the Universal Forest. I was deep in thought, searching for the right words. Imagine Rabbitskin's disappointment when he discovered I was the long, lost Creator.

When we reached the West River, we sat on the grassy bank and listened to the rushing rapids. The sound of water splashing against the river rocks soothed my racing mind. A cool breeze bounced off the Canyon Wall, making whispering sounds as it passed.

"Mr. Spencer," Rabbitskin finally said. "Something transpired on your trip, didn't it? Something that affects the Carnavorines. Let's not dilly-dally around. What happened, sir?"

I looked at Rabbitskin. His wrinkled face was filled with kindness. Although he was up in years, his big blue eyes still had the sparkle of a child. I lowered my head and began telling my tale. For some reason, I couldn't look at my friend.

Step by step, I told Rabbitskin about my trip to the future. I can't imagine what he was thinking while I was spilling the beans. Long after the last word was spoken, I was still afraid to look up.

I anxiously waited for a response.

After what seemed like an eternity, I couldn't take it anymore, and peeped up at the apeman. Rabbitskin sat motionless, withdrawn. I'd never seen him like this. He always had an answer for everything.

"I'm sorry," I said. "None of this makes sense."

"No," the apeman replied. "It makes perfect sense. Think about it. The Protectors love you. This is no small thing. They live only to serve the Carnavorines. That's why Yora and Tanjo are so fond of you. You're one of us. You're the creator."

Rabbitskin started sobbing. I gave him time to get it all out.

"Are you okay?" I eventually asked.

"I'm okay," he said, sniffing. "Do you want some trout, sir? If so, please allow me to catch them. You didn't do so well the last time we were here."

We both cracked up and began laughing. I guess nothing slips by a Carnavorine.

I leaned back on the grass, cupped my hands behind my head, and gazed into the sky. I only had one question for the apeman.

"What does it mean to be a creator?"

Rabbitskin laid down beside me, and assumed the same position.

"Being a creator holds the highest honor, young lad." he told me. "There's none higher. The most important thing I can tell you is, being a creator doesn't make you superior to your creations. You must have humility, sir."

Rabbitskin paused. He was thinking of a better explanation.

"Think of a mother," he finally said. "Does she feel more important than her child? A child that she created? Of course not. She only feels love."

I smiled as I thought of his loving example.

"May I be so bold as to offer an opinion, sir?" Rabbitskin asked.

"That's why we're here."

"It's The Three," the apeman said. "Let's place ourselves in their shoes. Maybe then we can see through their eyes."

"What do you mean?" I asked.

"It's simple," he told me. "The Three haven't created anything. Isn't that what really fuels their rage?"

"Go on," I said.

"Wasn't it Harry who invented Foxtronics, and wasn't he the one who harnessed the Power of Zero? The other three chaps have been riding his bloody coattails."

"How's that?" I questioned.

"Harry's the only real creator of the Godlings," Rabbitskin pointed out. "The Three's anger is not only aimed at us, lad, it's pointed at Harry, as well. I think it has been for a long time."

Rabbitskin was right. The Three had to be jealous of Harry. How could they not be? They must've felt inferior watching him create worlds all those years. He basically did it all by himself. Between Harry and the Carnavorines, they were probably devoured by envy.

I'd brought Rabbitskin to the river expecting a long, drawn-out lesson about creating life. Instead, the apeman explained creation with a single word — love.

Although time was critical, we didn't leave right away. I needed more time to clear my head. Who knows, maybe I could coax Rabbitskin into telling a story or two.

Chapter 27

I wasn't at the Green House tour, but Harry sent us a message while we were at the West River. I thought I'd share it with you, so you can better understand the big picture.

From the time The Three entered the Green Houses, they were in heaven. As instructed, Babbleskin poured it on thick. Everything was at their disposal, and not a single question went unanswered. The Carnavorine's operation could easily hold their attention indefinitely. Each individual creation chamber was enormous, and there were hundreds of them along the cave floor. Most of the Green Houses were assigned to manufacture one specific creation. Others were merely incubation chambers that didn't require constant watching or attention.

A total of 111 Carnavorines were assigned to man the operation. It was always that specific number. The apemen and apewomen roamed freely throughout the Green Houses, working by instinct alone, creating lifeforms to populate the universe. There's a narrow margin between life and death. To walk this line was to waltz on a whisk of wind.

Harry said it was like watching a colony of ants, each laboring individually, but all working for the greater good. He told me that they had impeccable rhythm and were synchronized to perfection.

As for the ambushed Carnavorine workers, you can imagine their surprise when the King and his entourage suddenly stumbled upon them. There was no time to warn these poor workers. I can only guess what they were thinking when they saw the unannounced circus moving through their sacred sanctuary.

Remember, these Carnavorines weren't observers, they were creators. None had ever even seen a human before. Humans had been manufactured long ago, way before their time.

Humans had thrived on Earth for many years, so, logically, none had been manufactured since. Don't forget, after species were created, they were left to do as they pleased. The fate of each species was determined by Mother Nature, not the Carnavorines. The apemen would never recreate a species Mother Nature chose for extinction. Each species only had one shot.

Only a few observers such as Rabbitskin, who were assigned to Earth, had seen a human. The rest had only heard of them by word of mouth, tales, or rumors.

Little did these Carnavorines know, Harry and The Three weren't humans. They were only look-a-like gods. It was probably best the workers didn't know their true identity. They would've soiled their britches, if they were wearing any.

Babbleskin led the three Godlings around from building to building. They couldn't wait to see what was next, but not Harry.

During the eye-opening tour, a new emotion began to emerge inside my father — guilt. How had he let his heart get so overrun with jealousy? Harry began to see the Godlings as their true selves. All of a sudden, he was disgusted by them. Maybe it's because he'd finally found his heart, or maybe, it was because when he looked at them, he saw himself.

While my father struggled with his guilt, The Three were happy and content wandering through Green Houses. My plan was working perfectly. The last thing on their minds was me.

I know what some of you are thinking. Why would we give The Three an all-access pass to the Green Houses? Wouldn't that be too risky? The answer is, no.

You see, the Carnavorines and I knew something that The Three would never understand. It didn't matter what they were shown inside the Green Houses. They could be handed a lifetime membership to the damn place, but it wouldn't do them any good. Making lifeforms was purely instinctive. It'd be easier teaching a cow to fly. Trillions of years, and they still couldn't get that through their thick skulls.

It's really cut and dry. The Three would never be able to create lifeforms, and the Carnavorines would never be able to create worlds. Even in the upper tiers of immortals and creators, there's a balance, no different than the balance of nature in any given circumstance. Big or small, the balance never changes. Even so, there's always one exception. There always is — me.

After my visit with the Other Me, I was beginning to possess the knowledge, instincts, and know-how of both races. Without so much as stepping foot inside the Green Houses or ever manufacturing a single pebble, I was beginning to unravel the secrets of The Four and the Carnavorines.

In basically one week, I'd gone from being a mere businessman to the creator of all things. I don't mean to complain, but I didn't exactly volunteer for the job. As you've heard, it was pretty much thrown into my lap.

I could've made myself known to you in many different ways. I chose this way to pack the most punch, and more important, to get rid of all the Maze-Os at the same time.

Why do you think I blew up Preotec? All traces of this technology had to be eliminated. The Power of Zero was never meant for humans. It should've never been introduced to you in the first place. Besides, it was only used to test my abilities.

Blowing up Preotec had to be done. I told you from the beginning sometimes people with certain knowledge have to make desperate decisions. Let me make myself clear — I don't have to be sitting here in this straitjacket. With my abilities, getting out of these restraints would be no challenge for me. Trust me, I could snap my finger and make your world dissolve like hot butter. Your fate, however, is not in my hands.

Remember, I didn't create you — the Carnavorines did.

That's why your fate will be determined by them alone.

The one thing that I learned during all this; I didn't need to create worlds or living organisms. That was the job of The Four and the Carnavorines, and like the Carnavorines, I wouldn't interfere with my creations either. For the Circle to work properly, I had to let my creations evolve naturally, too. One day I'll have the power to create The Four and the Carnavorines, but that's all I needed to do. I didn't micromanage Preotec, and I wasn't going to micromanage the universe. That's just good business sense.

Why in the hell do you think I blew up corporate headquarters, not the Carnavorines — the Sacred Laws. They can't interfere with you, but I can; and I did.

I'm a Carnavorine, but I'm also a Godling. I had to restore balance. Unlike the Carnavorines, The Four have no Sacred Laws. I did what needed to be done to right the ship.

Nonetheless, you're still not out of the woods quite yet.

Even now as you're hearing this broadcast, you're being observed closely. Make no mistake about it, you're currently being judged for your actions — and hanging me this morning probably wasn't a good start.

Chapter 28

Rabbitskin and I didn't want to leave the West River, but we eventually forced ourselves up, and started walking back.

Once on the Perigon Trail, a worrisome dread began to burden my thoughts and weigh down my spirit. I walked with a sagging head, dragging my feet from the stress. My legs were fighting a losing battle. They realized they were leading me straight into the lion's den.

Rabbitskin was suffering the same symptoms. A mournful mist lingered in the air, and a dark cloud followed our every move. We trudged painfully forward.

As we made our way down the trail, something began rustling inside the nearby forest. There were murmurs in the woodlands, calls from the underbrush, and the pitter patter of footsteps. The Universal Forest was crawling with activity.

Several times I whipped around to see what was stirring, but the noise would always stop. This annoying routine repeated itself all the way to the grasslands.

Once we were halfway across the field, I couldn't take it anymore. I turned and screamed, "Show yourself!"

Just like that, from out of nowhere, animals of all shapes and sizes burst from the surrounding forest. Flocks of birds used to populate faraway worlds gathered in uncountable numbers. A starburst of color filled the sky, changing hues with each subtle shift.

Land creatures began streaming in from the nearby woods and massing in great migratory herds. There were jaguars, bears, and hyenas from planet Earth's environment. There were skimsnakes, floons, and jogglegoats from Black River Hollow. From Deep Crater, oskars, blueboys, and muffletops were running around everywhere, and the list went on and on.

Although I'd never laid eyes on them, I knew every creature by name and region. Oddly, no species was a stranger to me.

At first Yora and Tanjo crouched in attack positions ready to trounce, but gradually they seemed to understand and relax.

The creatures had somehow known to congregate to this place, at this time. Maybe their convergence was born of instinct, or maybe just plain horse sense. Whatever the reason, they were here now.

All at once, the birds overhead flew down and perched in trees at the edge of the field, and every creature stopped where they stood. The Rainbow Butterflies left the roses and scattered equally among the animals.

It appeared I had Garden Valley's undivided attention.

"Well, go ahead," Rabbitskin whispered.

"Go ahead and do what?" I whispered back.

"I believe they're waiting for instructions, young lad," he said. "It seems we have new allies in our endeavors."

Looking across the field, something dawned on me. The upcoming battle wasn't only about me, the Godlings, and the Carnavorines. These animals had a right to fight for their existence as much as we did.

Suddenly, a white hark from the all-bird planet Fethar took to the sky. It was Keeya — the bird queen. She cried out from the heavens, zigzagging across the sky with outstretched wings, darting back and forth over the animal parade at blinding speeds.

Without warning, Keeya changed course and made a beeline straight for me. Upon arrival, a powerful push from her muscular wings eased her onto my right shoulder. Her 36-inch razor-edged talons reached well beyond my waistline, as she glared piercingly forward. The bird queen stretched her neck high and let out a bone-chilling shriek. The blast sent shock waves throughout the valley echoing many times before subsiding in a faint, reverberating hiss. All of a sudden, a paralyzing stillness hovered stagnate in the air.

I glanced up at the Keeya perched on my shoulder. I realized she'd landed there for a reason. She was the greatest hunter in the bird kingdom, but not today. Today she was a simple messenger; a flawless interpreter with rocket speed. The feathered warrior stood as a sculpture, eagerly waiting for her orders. I began to speak to her in the language of the hark.

"Fhofho fhir fher fhok fols fhey flok flok flok fa fe fort flik flik fotflor," I softly whistled. "Flea fay fly. Flea fay fly. Flea fay fly."

Keeya cocked her head from side to side, as I continued chanting instructions. When I was finished, she hurled herself up into the air. The wind from her gigantic wingspan blew back my hair, and every creature watched in awe as she swooped over the field of animals.

With unlimited projection, the great hunter screeched out continual high-pitched squawks. Far below, her captive audience listened to every squeak and shrill. Once she was satisfied my message had been received, she jetted away to complete her next assignment.

"Forgive me, sir," Rabbitskin said, watching her disappear. What's going on?"

"She's going to send my message to all the creatures of Rabistca," I said, staring at the sky where she'd vanished. "First, she'll fly to the Black Willow Swamp, then to the Jimini Jungle. Afterwards, she'll soar across water and sand until every Carnavorine creation has heard the battle call."

"Forgive me once again, sir," Rabbitskin said. "Did you say the Black Willow Swamp?"

"It's okay," I told the worried apeman. "All animals will unite on this day. Every creature of Rabistca will come together for the sake of survival. I've declared a planetary truce. It's not my words, however, that steer their actions; it's their own hearts. Rest easy, my friend; the Sacred Laws have not been broken. They come on their own free will."

Rabbitskin looked over the valley.

Tree tigers stood next to spotted deer; sway-hawks next to field mice. Bighorns strolled alongside moss-toes. Fig-frogs sat on top of branch-snakes. Throughout the valley, prey and predators stood together as one.

I'd given Keeya clear-cut instructions. Creatures from the Black Willow Swamp and Jimini Jungle would join together and migrate to Garden Valley. Some would come by wing, others by hoof. Some would crawl, a few would even slither. The Perigon Trail would soon be stuffed with every critter, varmint, and beast imaginable.

Larger animals who couldn't fit through the Slender Gap would have to take the more difficult road across the Lost Canyon Trail. Naturally, some creatures wouldn't be required to make the trip, like mothers nursing their young or aquatic animals. Only the strong and swift would travel on this dangerous quest.

"Make sure the slyths, dinosaurs, and the entities of the Black Willow Swamp are the first to be notified," I stressed.

Some of these long-forgotten, malformed mutants had developed special powers that might come in handy in a pinch. There was no telling what kind of vile and hideous things would scratch and claw their way out of the primitive swamp.

There was no time for the animals from the desert region to make the trip. Nevertheless, they were ordered to gather at the Solar Dunes of Monistory in case we needed them. The towering, rocky dunes were known by every creature dwelling in the dusty, dry region. It was home to the Mill Pond, the largest watering hole of the sweeping sands. It was the diamond of the desert.

It goes without saying that the mud-mouths, sharks, and other aquatic predators of the water region could do little to help. Regardless, I'd directed Keeya to fly to Merit Bay, the home of the flat-headed muzzle dolphin. These swift mammals could dive deep and spread my word fast. From the shallow bait-rich bayous of Bottle Bay to the dark ocean floors of Fathom Reef, anything that swam would hear the battle call. Like the desert, the ocean would be ready if called upon.

Something told me the water-world wouldn't be needed. If this war was going to happen, it would be fought on land. The Three had no power over water. They didn't create it.

Remember what Rabbitskin had said. "The Carnavorines weren't only masters of making living organisms, but livable environments, as well." That includes water.

The great oceans, lakes, and rivers of the universe were formed through years of sweeping rains, brought about by conditions created from the apemen themselves. Even the very air we breathe derives from wondrous plants and greenery used to populate their worlds.

Wind, rain, and snow were made by the apemen; sun, moon, and earth by The Four. This deadly duel would be a clash of the elements.

I really wanted to prevent this fight, and my heart told me I could. Unfortunately, my brain was always right, and it was telling me to batten down the hatches.

To be honest, I wasn't sure how any of these brave animals could help against a force as superior as The Three. Maybe they couldn't help at all, but they had assembled in Garden Valley for a reason, and I had complete faith in their instincts.

Garden Valley; all roads lead there. Ever since I first laid eyes on the place, something seemed to click. This had to mean something. Even during my trip to the future, the Other Me had revealed himself in the Garden. He did everything but draw me a freaking map.

Rabbitskin listened carefully as I described the hectic events now taking place across his home planet. He was floored by my perfect descriptions of places I'd never been and animals I'd never seen. His eyebrows shifted up and down as he clung to every word. As the story unfolded, his facial expressions went through a whole series of different inquisitive looks. He went from serious to surprised. From surprised to laughter, from laughter back to serious. There was a flood of emotions.

By the time I'd finished, Rabbitskin understood the magnitude of what was happening. Several hours later, reality set in.

The first wave of the speedy birds and flying creatures were now zooming over Cloud Canyon into the garden. The migration was moving full steam ahead. The next wave to hit would be the fastest of land animals. Cheetahs, spring-legs, and the elusive Velociraptors would be the first to arrive.

Although the dinosaurs on Earth had long perished, the ones left on Rabistca had not. They were now few in numbers, but some had managed to survive in the Forest section of the Carnavorine planet.

Rabbitskin drew a mental image of how the landscape might look tomorrow.

For the first time in his life, he was afraid.

Chapter 29

Back at the Green Houses, for countless hours, The Three were shown every nook and cranny of the operation. Trying to buy time, Babbleskin went into great detail describing everything under the sun.

At first, they couldn't believe their good fortune. Little by little, though, their enthusiasm began to waver. No matter how much information they received, they still didn't get it, none of it. They were no closer to the prize than they were when they started the tour. The Three tried to play it cool, but they were boiling inside. Bitterness turned into rage. Our plan was failing.

Babbleskin couldn't sense this, but Harry could. Knowing things were about to get ugly, he sprang into action.

"Hey," he whispered to Mrs. Malone, motioning her to lag behind.

Harry secretively looked around, pretending to make sure no one was listening.

"Can you believe how easy this is?" Harry said under his breath. "For years we've waited. Now we know."

"You understand this?" she whispered back.

"Of course, I do."

Excited, Mrs. Malone sprinted over to Ben and Mr. Malone and quietly passed on this information. They looked over and gave Harry a congratulatory nod of approval. From that moment on, The Three's attitude totally changed.

Harry was relieved but knew this was only a temporary fix. He immediately contacted us by Maze-O. His message was simple — *Urgent, hurry back!*

Harry was right. Thinking that he had obtained the Carnavorine's secrets, The Three would soon find a way to end the tour. Once they had Harry alone, they'd want to know what he knew; but he didn't know a damn thing.

We had to hurry before they called his bluff.

Chapter 30

When Rabbitskin received Harry's message, he abruptly stopped what he was doing and whistled for Yora and Tanjo to get ready for immediate departure.

"Be ready to run like the wind," he told them in his native tongue.

"Mr. Spencer!" Rabbitskin frantically yelled. "We'll make better time if you'll please allow me to assist you again. Mr. Spencer? Sir?"

Rabbitskin turned to see that I'd somehow snuck down into the valley of animals. I was now far away, gently stroking the thick fur of a 12-horned mountain ram. The puzzled apeman couldn't figure this out. Seconds earlier, I'd been standing right behind him. Concerned, he bolted down the hill toward my location.

"Logan!" Rabbitskin shouted as he ran down the grassy slope. "Didn't you receive Harry's message, sir? We must leave at once, young lad. Time is of the essence."

I continued stroking the purple mane of the unusual ram.

"Why do you think the animals are here in Garden Valley?" I calmly asked Rabbitskin when he arrived. "Why are they gathering?"

"I'm listening, sir."

"The animals didn't come here to pay homage to me," I told the apeman. "They've come to fight."

"I never thought I'd see war come to my home planet," Rabbitskin admitted. "I've seen many wars over the past 600 years. I've watched humans commit atrocious acts against one another. I always thought it was so senseless and barbaric. But now I see."

"See what?" I curiously asked.

Rabbitskin walked closer and began to pet the mountain dweller.

"Some things are worth fighting for," he said. "Some things are worth dying for."

This got me thinking. In the history of the Carnavorines, they'd never been in a single battle. They had no enemies; well, The Three, but they weren't aware of them until recently. Why didn't they have enemies? Simple. They didn't breed any. Or did they?

The human race was starting to scare the apemen. That's why Rabbitskin personally took on the task of watching humans himself. He was second in command of the Carnavorines and wasn't required to go on such assignments.

Humans were evolving in all the wrong ways. If they would've worked together, they could've gone far, but they didn't. They spent more time destroying than creating. Consumed by greed and the lust of money, one of their ridiculous inventions, they never achieved their true potential. That is, until Harry and I came along.

The Carnavorines had been watching closely since the Maze-O was revealed to the world. It took them many years and hundreds of Council meetings to finally approve Rabbitskin's introduction to us.

For the future survival of their race, Babbleskin declared a self-defense decree. Remember, the only way the Carnavorines could interfere with one of their creations was self-defense. The Council voted unanimously that our invention was evolving in such a way that it might one day harm the Carnavorines.

They were right, you know. If human technology would've ever advanced enough to travel to Rabistca, no matter what their original intentions, they would've eventually tried to conquer the planet. The Carnavorines knew this for a fact. They'd been watching humans from the beginning. Rabbitskin once told me that humans were unpredictable. Sadly, that's not true. Humans are very predictable.

As Rabbitskin and I continued to pet the ram, there was a long period of silence.

"Don't worry," I finally said. "I have a plan."

Right before Rabbitskin's eyes, I disappeared.

The apeman looked around in disbelief.

"Hey!" I screamed.

Responding to my voice, Rabbitskin turned to see me sitting on top of a large bull elk at the opposite end of the field. He started to walk toward me, but before he took his first step, I vanished again.

"Over here!" I shouted.

Rabbitskin turned toward the Universal Forest. I was now sitting on a crooked limb of an oak tree. I playfully waved up the hill at the apeman.

"What's going on, sir?" he yelled down into the valley.

Suddenly, there was a strong tap on Rabbitskin's shoulder. The apeman almost came out of his fur, leaping high into the air.

"Relax," I told him. "It's just me."

"Young Mr. Spencer," Rabbitskin said, trying to catch his breath. "Could you please refrain from doing that, sir? Need I remind you I'm 937-years-old. That's much too old for such tomfoolery."

"I'm sorry," I said, smiling. "But I needed to get my point across."

"Well, I can assure you, young lad," Rabbitskin replied. "You've made your point. I believe an explanation is in order, sir."

The idea first came to me when I was traveling inside the cosmic ray watching the Rainbow Butterflies. As they flew in slow motion, they left tiny tubular traces of colored light. The light was brighter just behind their wings, but as the beam lengthened, it gradually faded and eventually dissipated. Or maybe it didn't. Maybe it continued but wasn't visible to the human eye.

In science, if one peels back enough layers, they'll find more and more interesting stuff. In this case, you might say I hit the scientific jackpot. I discovered the Oh-Philly-Oh Tube. The Other Me had sent the Rainbow Butterflies with me to the future for a reason. I should've known.

I named the phenomenon after this geek who used to sit behind me in Physics class, Jack Gerds from Philadelphia. He sure didn't belong at Harvard. Coincidentally, the day he was enrolled, the college broke ground on a new multi-million-dollar laboratory on the east side of campus; the Jack Gerds Institute of Advanced Studies. Imagine that.

Anyway, Jack was always bothering the shit out of me, asking me to explain this or that. Every time I'd reluctantly give him an answer, he always had the same stupid response — "Oh." Like he knew what the hell I was talking about. Trust me, he didn't have a clue. The boy had the mental capacity of a worm.

Being from Philadelphia, he soon was given the nickname Oh-Philly-Oh. It stuck to him like glue. I always liked the name, just not him. At least now he'd be good for something.

I began describing to Rabbitskin how the Oh-Philly-Oh Tube worked. I told him I was now able to form enough molecular energy from inside my own body to form a cosmic ray. Once inside the ray, I could expand the size of the tubular traces of light and travel inside them. This would enable me to transport myself through the Oh-Philly-Oh Tube. Getting to specific locations was simple molecular calculus. I went into great detail of how light, energy, and matter could be manipulated using Harry's Power of Zero. I could've gone on for days.

After nodding and pretending to understand for a while, Rabbitskin stopped me in mid-sentence.

"Forgive me for being a ninny, sir," he said. "But I'll have to take your fine word for it. You're taking me places where my mind surely can't travel, young lad."

We both began laughing, but it was brief.

Suddenly, there was a thunderous sound coming from behind us. Some unknown force was moving through the Rainbow Roses and heading in our position. It sounded like an army approaching. The unmistakable sound of heavy feet stomping dirt was pounding the ground. The stampede grew louder until the entire valley began to shake. Every animal in the valley became antsy, and Yora and Tanjo were going nuts.

A huge dust cloud lifted high above the garden, but I could still see the tops of the Rainbow Roses being jostled side to side. Whatever was coming was big, and there were lots of them. I kept my eyes fixated on the dust cloud, expecting the worst. It wouldn't be long now. The oncoming storm was almost on top of us.

Then it happened.

Hundreds of saber-toothed tigers punctured through Rainbow Roses at full speed. It was the Protectors. They'd come to join us. When the cats reached our position, they slid to a screeching halt.

Like great bronze statues, the cats stood shoulder to shoulder, panting and out of breath. Thick smoke poured from their overworked lungs as they opened their mouths wide, fully exposing their razor-sharp tusks. The Protectors knew the Carnavorines were in trouble and were here to help.

Yora and Tanjo ran around in tight circles, growling with glee. They eagerly looked at Rabbitskin, trying to gain permission to join their brothers and sisters. Rabbitskin whistled his approval in his native tongue. The Protectors happily jumped in line, meshing with their friends.

Enamored by the prehistoric beasts, the animals in the valley began to stomp their hoofs, grunting and snorting in delight. The birds of the forest took flight and flew low over the tigers. The sound of their whistles and squawks rang across the valley. After a few minutes, the noise began to fade, and the birds flew back to the trees. Garden Valley became quiet again.

Suddenly, I heard a faint cry coming from the direction of the Rainbow Roses.

"Rabbitskin!" Someone shouted in the distance.

"Can anyone hear us?" Another voice chimed in.

"We're here!" Rabbitskin shouted back.

We couldn't see them, but we both recognized their voices. It was Bowskin and Fellskin. The two exhausted Carnavorines stumbled past the last row of roses and collapsed to their knees. They could go no farther. Trying to keep pace with an army of Protectors running at full speed was no easy task, even with a 10-foot stride.

"Let's see if they're okay," I said, laughing.

We rushed to check on our friends, who were still on their knees sucking wind. They were a mess. Their hair was in knots, and both were plastered with rose pedals. They looked like two psychedelic fur balls. Thankfully, the Rainbow Butterflies were down in the valley with the rest of the animals. They would've only added to the humiliation factor.

Fellskin clumsily pulled himself off the ground and onto his feet.

"We didn't know what to do," he said, panting. "It happened so--"

In the midst of trying to explain himself, Fellskin had finally come to his senses long enough to look around. He grabbed Bowskin by the arm and pulled him to his feet. The two Carnavorines scanned the horizon with mouths wide open.

Rabbitskin and I turned around to enjoy the moment with them. I noticed a few spring-legs had dribbled into the crowd. They were the fastest runners on Rabistca and could easily jump over small trees. The swiftest forest dwellers of the Jimini Jungle were beginning to arrive.

The arrival of the spring-legs only reminded me of what would be arriving soon; the eyeless creatures of the Black Willow Swamp. I didn't know why they were so important to me. I'd never even seen one of the beasts, but something told me they'd play a crucial role before this was over. That's why I'd given my messenger hark a very important task, an extra assignment before the giant bird would be relieved from her duty.

When Keeya was finished spreading my message, she was to return to the Black Willow Swamp to be a personal guide for these sightless mythical beings. Returning in a timely manner would be no problem for the swiftest of all Carnavorine creations. Keeya could cruise at speeds exceeding 900 miles per hour, not to mention soar to heights of 80,000 feet.

Once back at the swamp, I'd instructed her to fly slow along the Perigon Trail sounding her mighty voice. She would act as a beacon for the blind beasts to safely travel to our meeting grounds.

I have to admit, I was anxious to see one of the unusual creatures, but it'd have to wait. I needed to talk to Harry. He had some valuable information stored in that big brain of his; information that I currently needed.

I was glad that Fellskin and Bowskin had come to Garden Valley. They could help me test the Oh-Philly-Oh Tube.

All of these components were key parts in a new-developing, master plan — a plan that was about to go into effect, immediately.

Chapter 31

I told Rabbitskin to give the two Carnavorines the short version of what was going on, just the skinny.

The apeman led his two friends down into the valley to enlighten them. I wished I could've gone. I would've loved to see their reaction as Rabbitskin was relieving their curiosity; however, I needed to talk to Harry.

I sent my father a message over the Maze-O — *Contact me when you're alone.*

I'm alone now, he instantly replied.

Where are you? I asked.

Back in our room, he said. *Inside the Golden Band.*

Where are The Three? I messaged.

In their room, Harry messaged back.

An opening immediately formed in the Golden Band in Harry's room, and in walked me. I walked straight over and placed my hand on my father's shoulder, and before he could speak, we were back in Garden Valley.

Strangely, once we appeared, Harry didn't even bat an eye. For some reason, he wasn't thrown off by what had just happened.

"Let's take a ride," I told him. "We have a lot of catching up to do."

"Shea shik shy shoy si," I called out to Yora and Tanjo.

The two Protectors rushed to our sides.

Harry nonchalantly leaped onto Tanjo as if he was mounting his old horse Honey. My approach was much less dramatic. Yora kneeled and I clumsily scooted onto her back. Harry had always been the better cowboy.

I instructed the Protectors to carry us down to where the Perigon Trail opened into Garden Valley. I wanted to see the animals rolling in from the jungle. As soon as we arrived, two Velociraptors leaped from the trail. Yora and Tanjo didn't budge. My planetary truce was written in stone.

I didn't have time to explain everything to Harry in words. Unlike Rabbitskin, who needed caressing, Harry was only interested in facts.

"Close your eyes," I told my father.

Using our Maze-Os, I showed Harry everything that happened since I'd left Sina. It only took seconds. He could absorb information instantaneously.

Harry's eyes popped wide open.

"Of course," he said. "It couldn't be any other way."

Then Harry did something I didn't expect. My father let out the biggest sigh of relief I'd ever heard. It was like a trillion years of air was being pushed from his lungs.

I understood his reaction.

On Earth, humans tear their souls apart trying to figure out where they come from. Harry had carried the same burden, but not for a mere 70 or 80 years. His torment had lasted for an eternity, a billion human lifetimes. I couldn't imagine his toil.

Harry's reaction was more than relief; it was a total transformation. Right before my eyes, my father's face began to rapidly change. The heavy bags beneath his eyes and the deep crevices across his face tightened, smoothed, and vanished. His clumpy gray beard all but disappeared until I could clearly see a smile hidden beneath the once-matted mess.

Harry looked like he'd taken a long bath in the fountain of youth. He looked young, vibrant, and healthy. This time, he had truly let go. All the hate and jealousy had been flushed from his body, and the nasty demon living inside him, had been permanently excused.

Harry sat atop Tanjo like a young prince. He should've been happy, but strangely, he stared at me with a menacing glare.

"Sorry son, but there's something I have to do now," he said, in a stern voice.

"What?" I cautiously asked.

"This!"

Harry reached down, grabbed Tanjo by his mane, and gave him a hard kick in the side.

"Yee haw!" he yelled, blasting up the hillside.

What the hell, I thought.

"Come on, Yora!" I shouted.

"Yeeeeeeeeee haw!" I screamed, not to be out done.

Harry and I chased each other around the valley like we didn't have a care in the world. Our hoots and hollers, though, didn't go unnoticed. Rabbitskin and his two kinsmen were now sprinting toward our position.

I was probably about to receive another lecture, and I was pretty sure the word "tomfoolery" would be tossed in the mix. I didn't care; we were having a ball.

"Sir Harry, you're looking well," Rabbitskin said, confused. "But how did you get here? Did something go wrong?"

Rabbitskin was showing signs of frustration. Every time he thought he had things figured out, everything would change. This was a good thing. If he couldn't figure out my next move, neither could The Three.

As we said our hellos, Fellskin and Bowskin sheepishly stood in the background. They couldn't bring themselves to make eye contact with me. They were obviously still reeling from their conversation with Rabbitskin.

I nudged Yora and pulled close to the frightened Carnavorines.

"Fellskin," I said.

"Sir?"

"Holding your tongue doesn't suit you," I told him. "You've been dying to be a part of this since the beginning, and here's your chance. Can I count on you?"

"Yes, sir!" Fellskin said.

"That goes double for me!" Bowskin added.

"Good," I said. "That's better."

Fellskin and Bowskin had been with us since the beginning. They were loyal, trustworthy, and always willing to volunteer their services. They'd earned the right to be there.

As the five of us stood together, I had another vision, or maybe it was merely a gut feeling; nothing more than an average man would feel on any given day. I looked around. Everything just seemed right.

Harry and Rabbitskin were laughing in the background, deep into an unusual discussion. Fellskin and Bowskin were displaying their new status, walking up the hillside to inspect the Protectors. They moved with a fresh sense of pride. The creatures of the valley were all working together, communicating in snorts and grunts. They playfully tested their skills while new arrivals integrated into the mix.

The Supar passed overhead, and I tilted my head back to reap the full benefits. Its warmth only added to my pleasure. The table was set. So was my team. These were the four I'd carry into battle. From this day forth, I'd refer to them as my Inner Circle.

I called Fellskin and Bowskin back down the hill for a meeting. Yora and Tanjo were sent to rejoin the Protectors. Once the apemen arrived, I asked everyone to form a circle and join hands. I got some weird looks, but they did it anyway.

"Close your eyes," I instructed.

I waited until every eyelid was shut good and tight.

"Okay," I said. "You can open them now."

Everyone eased their eyes open, and when they did, they could hear the distinctive sound of waves crashing against sand. We were standing on the beach near Harry's cabin. I'd brought us back to where it all began.

I did this for a specific reason; I needed to know if I could carry more than one person through the Oh-Philly-Oh Tube. Thankfully, my experiment was a success. As long as everyone was touching, it was possible.

Fellskin and Bowskin didn't seem to enjoy my little test. They each had a death grip on my hands, and I was sure my fingers were going to snap.

"Gentlemen," I said. "If you'd please allow some blood to return to my arms, we'll go inside the cabin and I'll explain everything."

The two embarrassed apemen dropped my hands and apologized.

As we were walking to the cabin, I glanced over at the Jimini Jungle. It was eerily quiet, altogether different than the first time I was there.

With the most dangerous predators on their way to Garden Valley, the smaller creatures could finally relax. What a relief it must've been not having "hot lunch" plastered across their backs. Without their usual warning yelps and squawks, the forest had become tranquil and untroubled.

Better enjoy it while it lasts, I thought in passing. Soon, it'd be back to the never-ending game of run for your fucking life.

We moved inside the cabin.

It was good to see Harry's old hangout again, especially for him. He bounced around picking up homemade wooden items that he'd carved. Once he'd made his rounds, he grabbed an antique rifle mounted over the fireplace and began thoroughly inspecting the barrel. The old log cabin wasn't much to look at, but it was special to my father and it showed.

I told everyone to grab a seat.

Harry and I pulled up a few chairs. Fellskin and Bowskin squeezed onto a couch and, as expected, Rabbitskin planted himself on the kitchen table. For some odd reason he liked that spot. I guess smooth wood against hairy butt feels nice.

When everyone was situated, I turned to my father.

"Harry," I said. "There's something I need to know. Something only you'd know."

"I'm listening."

"When we were at the Canyon Wall, we saw that slyth gobble you down. We also saw you reappear. As long as you've been around, this couldn't have been the first time you met your demise."

"Of course not," Harry told me.

"When it happens," I said, "how long does it take you to reform? Is it the same every time? Is it the same for The Three? How far away do you reappear from the original position of your death. How--"

"Hold on," Harry said, bringing my interrogation to a halt. "I get it. But I can only answer one question at a time. You see Logan, I only have one mouth. As good as you are at math, you should be able to grasp this concept."

Great, I thought, my smart-ass ways were beginning to rub off on my father.

Harry told us that The Four had met their doom many times in the past. It only began when they stumbled upon the Carnavorines and their unpredictable creations. Before that, they were in complete control of their surroundings.

The dinosaur days were especially hard on the Godlings. It took them years to adapt a new way of thinking, to become alert, aware. Although they'd always reform after each death, they didn't care for this phenomenon. It made them uneasy.

Harry said it'd take anywhere from five seconds to five minutes to reform after each fatality. They'd always reappear no more than a couple of miles from the original spot of their death, usually much less. Time and distance varied with each new episode.

"How many times has it happened to you?" I asked Harry.

"Two, three hundred, I suppose. Why?"

"And The Three?"

"About the same for each. What are you getting at, Logan?"

I paused for a moment. This was important for some reason. It was really important. It was. It waaas. "One thousand, one hundred and eleven!" I shouted, springing to my feet.

"That's the life-number for the Carnavorines," Bowskin said. "What's that got to do with anything?"

"Everything," I told him. "The life-number for the Carnavorines, is the death-number for The Four!"

It hit me like a ton of bricks. I now knew what had to be done. I also knew that the upcoming battle would be fought to the death, 1,111 deaths each, to be exact. No more games.

"The Three must die," I reluctantly told the group. "They'll destroy this universe and everything in it. Soon they'll find out about Harry's betrayal. Then it'll be too late. We must strike while the iron's hot, while the element of surprise is on our side."

All eyes went to Harry. The former member of The Four sat expressionless, glazed. This was his burden, his cross to bear.

"This is a sad day for me," Harry admitted, clearing the air. "But The Three's lust for power has crossed the line. There's no hope for them now. They must be stopped."

"Can it be done?" Rabbitskin asked.

"Maybe," he said. "But it won't be easy. One alone is a formidable foe, but together, they're almost unstoppable."

The room fell uneasily silent.

"Tell us what to do, young lad," Rabbitskin finally said, turning to me.

"Please, son," Harry agreed. "I'm in."

Harry was on board. Like me, he was a scientist, and facts were facts. He'd found his heart, and The Three had not. It was a hard pill to swallow, but it was really that simple.

"Okay," I said. "Listen up."

The blueprint for victory was simple; time for The Three meant death to us. To be clear, I emphasized this again. "Time for The Three means death to us!"

It'd take about a minute for any member of The Three to draw-in enough molecular energy to destroy the universe. That one-minute gap was crucial. That precious minute was the difference between life or death.

"We better make damn sure they don't get it!" I stressed. "And if The Three touch hands, it's over; period, done. We must keep them separated at all cost."

"How will we get them to Garden Valley?" Fellskin asked.

"The same way I got you here," I replied.

As usual, Fellskin and Bowskin looked lost. They tried to keep up, but always seemed to be a step or two behind. "Perpetually tardy," as Rabbitskin would've phrased it.

"After this meeting," I told Fellskin. "I'll transport you and Bowskin back to Garden Valley. Watch over the creatures. Prepare them for battle. When we arrive with The Three, everything will happen fast. Be ready for anything!"

"We'll be ready," Fellskin said.

"You can count on us," Bowskin added.

"Use Yora and Tanjo for speed and strength," I told the apemen. "Ride them as your battle stallions."

"What about me?" Harry asked.

"After we've dropped off Fellskin and Bowskin, "I'll transport you back to your room in Sina. Then I'll take Rabbitskin with me to the Halls of Goya to prepare for the meeting."

I closed my eyes and activated my Maze-O.

"I've just informed Babbleskin and Snakeskin that we'll be arriving soon. Harry, after you've returned, the King will send his committee to get the The Three. They'll come to your room, last. When you answer the door, they should be none the wiser."

As I continued revealing my plan, I could see tension growing on the faces of my Inner Circle. They could all add quite well. With my new-and-improved traveling abilities, we were only hours from the impending war.

Rabbitskin tried one last plea for diplomacy.

"Forgive me, good sir." the apeman said. "But the Carnavorines are great debaters and reasoners. Shouldn't we give the King and Council a final chance to rationalize with the Godlings? Maybe there's still an outside chance for a peaceful resolution."

"Rabbitskin, listen very carefully," Harry said, taking over the conversation. "The Three's rage has come to a head. Their patience is over. They hate you! They hate the Carnavorines! If they had your secrets, we wouldn't be having this conversation. You'd be dead. Your planet would be dust. And everything you've ever created would be obliterated."

There was nothing left for me to add.

In Carnavorine terms; if we hesitated, our roos was cooked.

Chapter 32

I excused myself from the cabin and wandered down the beach to the ocean's edge. I needed a moment to gather my thoughts. It felt nice removing my shoes and dunking my feet into the warm, salty water. I sucked in hard, filling my lungs with fresh sea air.

Along the seashore, thousands of sand fleas scurried in and out of the strong tide. Each played a never-ending game of hide and seek as they continually buried and unburied themselves in the ever-shifting sand.

Just offshore, a miniature-mouth seagull cried out. With stiffened, outstretched wings, he rode the steady breeze up and down like a kite. Eyeing a school of bait, the little seabird plunged into the water, practicing spearing minnows with his tiny, sharp beak. Due to the planetary truce he couldn't actually feed, but it didn't stop him from polishing up on needed skills. As the seagull repeated his routine, wave after wave rushed past my feet, sinking my toes farther into the sand.

What is it about an ocean? The sounds and smells are flawless ingredients to a perfect recipe. Throw in a sprinkle of sun and a dash of wind and it simply has no equal.

What a wonderful world the Carnavorines had created. The apemen were the world's finest artists, each carrying a magical brush. Every new canvas brought vivid colors and exceptional beauty, painted with love, signed with hope and understanding.

Everything on Rabistca had purpose and meaning. The largest dinosaurs and smallest insects all carried the same weight. That was the true treasure of the Carnavorines.

Back on Earth, Bigfoot was a joke to most people, a myth; a dirty, stinky hermit who lived in the shadows. How wrong humans can be sometimes. From where I stood, Bigfoot was the most glorious creature in the universe, each a Saint, all so beautiful.

I finally understood the Carnavorines, and I'd be damned if I was gonna let The Three harm any of their creations. This world deserved to live; all their worlds did.

All of a sudden, I felt eyes burning the back of my head. It was Rabbitskin and Harry. They'd come to dip their anxieties into the healing waters, too.

As the waves continued pounding the shoreline, the three of us stood together. I felt safe around Harry and Rabbitskin. They were my two best friends and the only family I'd ever known.

Rabbitskin had taught me well, and today it was time to graduate. He never succeeded in his quest to teach me manners, my potty mouth won that particular battle, but what he did teach me was love. I felt it on the beach that day, and it was more powerful than the mighty sea stretched out before us.

Chapter 33

As previously decided, our first stop was returning Fellskin and Bowskin back to Garden Valley. I couldn't believe how much the countryside changed during our brief absence. The animal population had nearly tripled. An endless stream of spectacular species was now cramming in from the overflowing Perigon Trail.

I wish I could've stayed to watch the growing spectacle. Instead, I grabbed Harry and Rabbitskin and transported us to our room in Sina.

"You know what to do." I said to Harry in a hurried voice.

"Yep," he replied.

"Then we'll see you at the Halls."

Wasting little time, I touched Rabbitskin's arm and transferred us to the Grand Arch of the Halls of Goya.

I'd seen the famed Arch in dreams and visions, but it didn't do it any justice. Rabbitskin was temporarily paralyzed, gawking upward in utter disbelief, dwarfed by the gigantic work of art. The crippling effect soon spread to me, and I stood stock-still, incapacitated by the sheer wonderment of the towering monument.

High above, a muffled chime sent an unwanted drop of water floating downwards. With a dull smack, it splattered against the hard surface near my feet, sending a reverberating plopping sound echoing through the halls. Only when the echo had barely faded, and the Arch was satisfied the coast was clear would it detach another droplet. This hollow repetitive tapping had a chilling effect, and the unceasing throb only added girth to the lump in my throat.

"Come on," I whispered.

As we tiptoed past the Grand Arch into the halls, even Rabbitskin's huge frame seemed to shrink into a childlike figure. Each new step brought another creepy, amplified thud that ricocheted deep inside the long chamber. I was afraid to talk, scared the slightest peep might shake the foundations of the ancient wonder, sending its giant columns crashing to the ground.

The Silver Stone had kept the Halls of Goya sealed for over a million years. Locked up airtight, the Carnavorine meeting place was perfectly preserved by its stubborn captor. There wasn't a speck of dust, mold, or mildew, not a single cobweb. Even the smallest spider couldn't squeeze past the impenetrable Menite. The handcrafted marble was still brilliantly polished and in its original state. We were standing in the middle of a time capsule.

Inside the Royal Chamber, the only source of light came from huge torches hung on each column leading to the Grand Council Room. Thankfully, Snakeskin set fire to them before our arrival. Without these flames, the halls would be as dark as the Black Willow Swamp itself.

As we crept past each magnificent pillar, our shadows turned into inky giants that clung to the walls, sometimes creeping as high as the 80-foot ceilings themselves. For lack of a better word, it was spooky.

When the burning torches flickered and danced, I could scarcely make out long-forgotten species carved into the marble supports. These godlike creatures had dragon wings and serpent eyes, long extinct like the craftsmen who chiseled them ages ago.

The lavish hall seemed to go on forever, and I began to wonder if we'd ever reach the end.

Finally, a loud voice called out.

"HELLO ello ello." It was Snakeskin. "Walk straight ahead. You're almost here ere ere."

Like two frightened children, we scurried past the last column and leaped through an open doorway. We'd made it to the Grand Council Room; a place where lost generations of Carnavorine kings came to share thoughts and ideas.

As soon as I entered the room, my arms and legs began to tingle and burn. My torso began to shift and sway. Something was tugging at me, pushing, pulling, shoving. I was no longer in control. I was in the clutches of the Spirit Kings.

Rabbitskin and the Council members watched in horror as my frame began violently twitching and jerking back and forth. Ancient Carnavorine ghost kings began running unchecked inside me, all from a different time, each with a different story. I began to see past kings as they sat in the Grand Council Room all those years ago.

I saw Goodskin, who wrote the Sacred Laws; Manskin, creator of the desert dragons; Horseskin, Wormskin, Lakeskin the rainmaker, and on and on.

My vision sailed further back in time. I saw myself. I saw the elated look on my face when I finally did it; one thousand, one hundred and eleven Carnavorines, all created in the same instance. It's how it had to be done.

The Four had once held their heads to mine, showing me their past. Now it was the Carnavorines' turn. The Spirit Kings were showing me their history, my history; our history.

These royal ghosts had been imprisoned inside these halls for an eternity, but they wouldn't allow themselves to simply fade. Instead, kept alive by hope, they patiently waited for this day to come, for this very moment. They'd been waiting for me.

When the Spirits exited my body, the ancient ghosts became visible to everyone in the room. One by one they swirled around us, flew upward, and vanished. The Spirit Kings had completed their mission. Their duty was done.

After the Royal Spirits passed, I fell to my knees. My strange encounter with the ghosts had left me dizzy and weak.

Rabbitskin ran to my side.

"Young Mr. Spencer! Are you okay?"

I collapsed to the floor.

Rabbitskin frantically grabbed the pouch Fellskin had given him back at the Old Oak. It contained water from the West River; known throughout Rabistca for its magical healing powers.

The apeman gently lifted my head and placed the nipple of the pouch against my lips. I opened my mouth wide and let the cool liquid trickle down my throat. It was working. The effects of the Royal Spirits were being flushed from my aching body.

I clumsily stumbled to my feet.

"Easy, sir," Rabbitskin insisted, clutching tight to my arm. "Take your time."

I struggled to find balance, but somehow managed to steady myself long enough to look around.

The Grand Council Room was much more streamlined than I expected. It was basically an enormous vertical cylinder with a U-shaped table in the center. Around the outside diameter of the table, 10 benches were sculpted into the floor. An 11th larger seat, obviously for the King, was arranged in the center.

As I've mentioned, the Halls of Goya were carved out of a single piece of pure goya marble. The Grand Council Room, however, was the heart of this legendary stone. The nucleus of the rare marble was no doubt the most beautiful section. The dazzling green and silver goya ran rampant here, creating breathtaking patterns that splattered from all angles. This was nature's version of an abstract painting, a Carnavorine Jackson Pollock original.

Hundreds of torches encircled the tube-like room, illuminating it to perfection. Approximately 10-feet high and only inches apart, each flame overlapped and burned as a singular ring of fire.

Overlooking the Council's table, embedded into the wall, was a Great Marble Throne. Never in my life had I seen such workmanship and detail. I rudely shoved my way past the Carnavorines to get a closer look.

The throne was a marvelous tribute to the finest Carnavorine creations. The talented sculptor had an artist's touch, an eye for trickery, and an acute attention to the smallest particulars.

The armrests were two Protectors leaping forward with claws and fangs fully exposed; a tribute to Cowskin, no doubt.

The backrest was a white hark's head with cold green eyes and an intimidating glare. Its large beak protruded outward, giving the great hunter a 3D visual effect. The queen of all birds looked ready to pounce on anything that dared move.

The throne's legs were a spectacular blend of predators chasing their prey of choice. A few of the fleeing animals seemed to melt right into the floor.

The seat was comprised of various snakes tightly braided into a remarkable web. Numerous snakes strayed from the throne and wandered onto the ground or slithered their way up the walls.

The Great Marble Throne had no straight lines, corners, or edges. It seemed to be alive, marble in motion. Hanging on the back wall, a massive torch lit the built-in chamber. This was no ordinary flame. It shot its fiery beam directly onto the throne below, causing it to glow fire-engine red. It burned with a devilish smoldering flare.

I edged closer. I had to. Something had a hold of me. I felt my feet lift off the ground. Apparently, all the ghosts hadn't left the chamber. One still remained.

As I was unwillingly pulled into the air, I finally mustered the courage to look up. It was the ghost of Skillskin who held me. He was the renowned king who first discovered the giant piece of goya marble in this hidden cave. This was his vision, his lifelong dream.

Since the Silver Stone appeared all those years ago, past kings had been secretly congregating inside the Halls of Goya. Maybe the Silver Stone wasn't so impenetrable after all. The strong Menite from Harry's home planet could hold back flesh, a proven fact; however, it wasn't intended to incarcerate the spirit world.

As I helplessly dangled overhead, something occurred to me. In an odd way, Harry's jealous intentions may have backfired. These imprisoned walls provided a pristine safe house for the departed kings, a sort of Restless Spirit Retirement Home. The Silver Stone was a perfect barrier between the two worlds. The dead wouldn't be bothered here. To them, it was a blessing in disguise.

By unanimous vote, the deceased kings had given Skillskin's spirit the distinct honor of placing the long-awaited Creator onto his rightful seat. This is what they'd been waiting for, the sole reason they'd remained.

After being positioned on the throne, I looked up at the ghost of Skillskin. I gave the King an appreciative smile. Satisfied, he waved, and slowly vanished. The last of the Spirit Kings could finally rest in peace.

From the moment I was placed on the throne, the flame above me began to dim. The temperamental torch was cooling. Seconds later, it was over. The Fiery Throne had been permanently extinguished. Its longtime rage had ended.

Chapter 34

Between Ghost Kings playing leapfrog through my body, and Skillskin's antics, the Council members had seen enough. The apemen fell to their knees. There was no doubt who I was.

I quickly took charge of the situation. There was no time for bows, speeches, or curtain calls. Babbleskin had contacted me by Maze-O. The Three were on their way.

I asked the Carnavorines to hurry and take a seat. After everyone had settled, there was an uneasy stillness. The air became chilled and stagnate. Our breath blew cold.

I looked at Rabbitskin. There was sadness in his face and worry. His friends, planet, and every Carnavorine creation could soon be gone. The end game was approaching.

Don't worry, I quietly mouthed.

I needed Rabbitskin to be his normal self, a rock. Now was the time for strength. Now was the time for courage.

"Time has run out," I told the Council. "Your past, present, and future are in peril. Even as we speak, The Three are approaching, but there will be no meeting here today."

The apemen began to grumble between themselves.

"Hold on!" I shouted, raising my voice over the crowd. "Hear me out!"

I hastily explained to the apemen what would likely happen if I allowed this meeting to take place.

First, The Three would take control and corner Harry about his knowledge of the Carnavorines' secrets. When that failed, they'd threaten the King, and when that didn't work, it was payback time. Not on my watch.

The Three wouldn't step foot in the Grand Council Room. Never! Matter of fact, they wouldn't make it past the Great Hall. The ancient meeting room was holy ground. They had no business there.

"Snakeskin," I said. "You and the rest of the Council come with me and Rabbitskin. Go to the first column near the Grand Arch. Hurry!"

As fast as their furry legs could take them, the apemen sprinted down the long hall. I hopped onto Rabbitskin's back and we followed suit. I didn't use the Oh-Philly-Oh Tube. Call me old fashioned, I still preferred traveling by foot. Not to mention, the piggyback ride was starting to grow on me. I had no more delusions about keeping pace with a Carnavorine.

When we arrived, I stood on Rabbitskin's shoulders, pulled the torch from the first column, and leaped to the ground.

How long will it take you to snuff these torches out?" I asked Snakeskin.

"Between the six of us, not long," he said.

"Work your way back to the Grand Council Room and put them out as you go," I instructed. "When you're done, stay put, stay silent, and keep out of sight."

"Not to second guess you sir," Snakeskin said, looking confused. "But without the torches, the halls will be as black as the Mud Pits of Prisuma."

"That's what I'm counting on," I told the apeman. "Move with purpose, my friend."

Snakeskin yelped out some bird sounds and the Carnavorines went to work. As they moved away from our position, the Great Hall turned darker and darker until all traces of light disappeared. The only thing saving us from total blindness was the lone torch I held in my hand, and even it struggled to shine.

Suddenly, Harry warned me over the Maze-O that The Three were close, but there was no need. I could hear muffled voices in the distance. I had to tell everyone my plan fast.

I snatched Rabbitskin by the arm and guided him back down the hall until we reached the 15th column. This should be far enough, I told myself. We crouched low and huddled tight.

I activated my Maze-O and relayed my plan to Rabbitskin, Harry, and Babbleskin. We were out of time. We had to move now. With torch in hand, Rabbitskin sprang to his feet. I stayed behind the marble support, tucked away in the shadows.

"Greetings!" Rabbitskin shouted, welcoming the oncomers. "Stay where you are, I'm coming your way."

I pushed my back hard against the pillar, tried not to breathe, and listened. I was nervous. I'd just made a last-minute change to my plan. If I was gonna pull this off, I'd need a "helping hand" from the King.

I slowly peeked around the corner.

From my position, Rabbitskin's torch did little good. I could only make out a few blurry figures. Their voices, however, rang clear in the sound-reflective chamber.

"Sorry, chaps, but the path ahead is dangerously dark," Rabbitskin informed the group. "I can assure you, though, once we've cleared the Great Hall, the Grand Council Room will be well lit. Logan and the others are waiting for us there."

"I can't see a damn thing," Harry said. Right on cue.

"So not to stray," Rabbitskin instructed, "We'll all join hands, and I'll give us safe passage."

The next part of plan was extremely important. We couldn't let The Three touch hands. We had to keep them separated.

Right away, Rabbitskin grabbed Ben's hand. Mr. Malone tried to follow, but Harry wedged himself between the two. Now it was Babbleskin's turn. He took Mr. Malone's hand and turned to my mother.

"My lady," he gently said, extending his gray, furry arm.

Mrs. Malone cracked a disingenuous smile, stalled, and suspiciously jerked her head around. Maybe she was sensing something. This could spell big trouble.

Come on, I thought. You can do it.

Finally, after a tense, extended pause, she reluctantly took the hand of the King.

Sunskin, Moonskin, and Lambskin didn't understand what was going on. I'd totally forgotten about them. The Carnavorines weren't a part of my scheme, and none had Maze-Os. I was about to broadcast a dire message to Rabbitskin, but he beat me to the punch.

165

"You three gents wait here," he told the apemen. "After I've led our guests safely through, I'll send Snakeskin for you."

It took a while, but the group slowly inched their way forward until they arrived at the column where I was hiding. I had to stay on my toes. The darkness was so intense, even at close range, I could barely make out each silhouette. So not to misstep, I counted each shaded figure until I reached six. That was the magic number. I pounced!

"Hello, mother," I said, locking onto her hand.

There were no more games, no more Halls of Goya, and no more secrets. We were all standing in the center of Garden Valley surrounded by my Animal Army.

Chapter 35

Everyone who passed through the Oh-Philly-Oh Tube was severely blinded by the sudden switch from darkness to light. Unable to see, The Three most likely had no idea where we were or what was going on. If I played my cards right, I could use this to my advantage. Realizing their vision would soon refocus, I had a tiny window of opportunity.

"Fellskin! Bowskin!" I desperately cried out.

Within seconds, from the haze came a rush of wind.

"Got ya," a friendly voice said as I was plucked from the ground.

Fellskin and Bowskin had been patrolling the valley on high alert, waiting for us to appear. Luckily, we punched through the Oh-Philly-Oh Tube near Fellskin and Yora. They quickly assessed my predicament and tore a path to my side.

My vision was still fuzzy, and I strained to get my bearings. I was getting worried. If I wasn't first to regain sight, the battle would be over before it began.

I should've known what Fellskin would do next. He had the same remedy for any situation, water from the West River. To Fellskin, the river water was aloe, antibiotics, hangover reliever, mouthwash, burn cream, and lotion all wrapped up into one. It was his Carnavorine cure-all. Today's use; prescription eye drops.

The apeman tilted my head back, forced my eyelids open, and splashed water across my entire face. In an instant, my vision was renewed.

I thought I'd prepared myself for what Garden Valley might look like upon my return. I was sorely mistaken. Scattered throughout the valley were creatures that words simply can't describe. For millions of years, Mother Nature had run wild inside the Black Willow Swamp. Without the Carnavorines' watchful eyes, evolution had turned their creations into slithery monsters the apemen themselves would no longer recognize. The long-hidden creatures were now mutated abominations of their original design.

I knew time was of the essence, but I simply couldn't peel my eyes away from these unusual beings. Even with the valley stuffed full of abnormal animals, the swamp creatures stood out.

There was one in particular that immediately grabbed my attention, maybe because it was so big, but probably because it was so close. It seemed to be part worm, part cricket, and part shark. My closest guess would be a Great White Wormicket.

This thing-a-ma-jig's enormous worm-like body was covered with gooey suction cups. What purpose they served was anybody's guess. It had many sets of appendages similar to the hind legs of a grasshopper. Of course, it had no eyes, but it had rows of razor-sharp teeth. Hundreds of red-plated gill slits were laced across the creature's back. Strangely, some were even on the monster's legs.

The Great White Wormicket could no doubt breathe on land or underwater. To hunt, I imagine it could swim, squirm, or jump extremely well. This vile, overgrown invertebrate was only one of a thousand outlandish beasts in Garden Valley to fight on our behalf.

The queen hark had done an amazing job guiding them to the valley unharmed. The blinding light threw off their highly developed radar and made them exceedingly vulnerable outside the protection of their shadowy realm.

Quite frankly, under such duress, I didn't know what role these kooky lifeforms could play. They looked so helpless away from their natural environment. That little voice inside my head, though, kept reminding me of their great importance, and it was screaming louder than ever.

I could've watched all day. It's not often the circus comes to town, but I was suddenly reminded that I had more pressing issues. Fellskin gave me a firm pop and suggested I might want to wake up. The Three were beginning to win back their sight.

Bowskin and Tanjo trotted up behind us. I acknowledged them with a slight nod, but my attention quickly turned to The Three. Thankfully, they were still half-blind, but I knew their recovery was near. I began to weigh my options.

First, I needed to familiarize myself with my new surroundings. With the constant influx of animals, the setting had changed quite significantly while we were away. No longer distracted by the creatures from the Black Willow Swamp, I took my first honest look around.

Fellskin and Bowskin had been busy arranging the battlefield during our departure. I must say, I was impressed.

Garden Valley was all flatland except for one gradual swell near the Rainbow Roses. That was now the Protectors' domain. Side by side, the edgy cats stood, growling, biting, snarling, pushing, and shoving. They were hoping for action, praying for it. The Protectors weren't intimidated. They were born to fight.

Between the Protectors and the creatures below, the apemen had cleared a long, narrow section of the field. It was 100% animal-free and stretched across the valley end to end. This would allow us to move unobstructed through the animal ranks.

Very clever, I thought.

Fellskin slid off Yora and began pouring river water into the eyes of Rabbitskin, Harry, and the King. Bowskin placed two fingers on his upper lip and loudly whistled. Three Protectors instantly broke ranks and stormed down the travel lane.

These weren't merely three randomly chosen cats; they were the cream of the crop, handpicked for their superior skills and years of proven success in ugly situations.

Yora and Tanjo were young and willing, but these were the most high-ranking and vicious Protectors in the kingdom. Rilo was chosen for Rabbitskin, Milra for Harry, and Hulljo for me.

Bowskin was about to whistle an order for Yollow, the King's personal Protector, when something happened no one could've predicted; a game changer.

From the far side of the field, a dark figure began creeping down the center of the cleared path.

"This can't be," Bowskin said, pulling close to me.

"What is it?" I whispered.

"It's Pattyon," he said. "Lord of the Protectors."

I'd never heard of Pattyon. All I knew was the biggest, baddest, meanest looking saber-toothed tiger I'd ever seen was heading straight for us.

From his birth, the apemen knew he'd be special. He was a Quizerant, a Carnavorine term used to describe a rare breed of Protector, a freak of nature. Only one was born every hundred generations.

Quizerants weren't bred by the Carnavorines. Most species eventually formed their own wonders, no different than an albino or a dwarf. If species flourished long enough, evolution would ultimately shape their future, and a Quizerant was the best evolution had to offer.

Their very existence was a miracle within itself. They had abnormally long lifespans, 10 times that of a Carnavorine. No one knew why. Like the creatures of the Black Willow Swamp, they couldn't be observed or studied; not a chance in hell.

Quizerants were always born male and always the same color, pure coal black. Their frames were much larger, claws sharper, and tusks longer than an ordinary cat.

Every creature in the valley froze in place as the rare oddity calmly strolled by. None had ever seen him. The few who had weren't around anymore. Normally, if Pattyon made his presence known, that was your ass.

Pattyon, like all Quizerants before him, had been a loner since birth. Untamable and unbreakable, he lived a life of solitude, lurking in dark places. Misunderstood and rarely seen, the mysterious cat had long faded into folklore. Until now he hadn't been spotted in more than 3,000 years.

As the Quizerant moved closer, I locked eyes with the beast, and as I did, I began to see his plight. I could actually read his mind. Pattyon had been watching me for a long time. Something had drawn him to the beach the day we arrived in Harry's cabin. He'd been tailing me since.

When I first walked up to the Jimini Jungle, he was prowling in the thick underbrush, studying my every move. As we traveled through the shine-vines he silently glided across the top of the ape-made tunnel. He beat us to the Black Willow Swamp. When Harry and I rode Yora up the Slanted Root, we unknowingly passed directly over him. He was securely attached to the underside of the leaning landmark.

When we encountered the slyth, Pattyon was only a stone's throw away, hidden, buried in the spongy moss. He shadowed us all the way to the Old Oak.

Even Yora and Tanjo with their remarkable sense of sight and smell didn't have a clue of his whereabouts. How could they? No creature alive could match the skills of a Quizerant.

After we entered Sina, Pattyon returned to Garden Valley. Like me, he felt an uncontrollable urge to go there. He had remained in the valley since, concealed high up in a giant live oak tree. From his secret perch, the Quizerant had been patient, watching events unfold. I guess he'd finally seen enough. Pattyon wasn't here to make trouble; he was here to carry me into battle.

I carefully eased off Yora and slowly walked up to the lethal cat. Garden Valley hung by a thread as I stood face to face with the legendary creature. Rabbitskin, Harry, and Babbleskin's eyes had been washed clean, and they, too, were fixated on us.

Pattyon stretched down, and I mounted the beast. As we rose together, the Quizerant let out an ungodly roar. His confident blast quickly spread to every animal in the overcrowded field, and they began to cheer. The ovation was so loud it shook the very ground beneath my feet.

As the cries, toots, and snarls reached a fever pitch, my inner circle became intoxicated with optimism. Motivated and filled with adrenalin, they enthusiastically climbed up on their warrior tigers.

There wasn't a second to spare.

The Three had recovered.

Chapter 36

Keeya returned to the sky, circling overhead. Her high-pitched screams punctured through the mounting tension which now blanketed the area like a low-laying fog. After many passes, she swooped down and once again returned to my shoulder. Upon her arrival, Pattyon let out another deafening roar. The battle call had been sounded.

Babbleskin hurried up the slope where the Protectors were stationed. There he'd find Yollow waiting for him. The aging King struggled onto his longtime Protector, positioning himself where he had a good view of the valley below.

It was only appropriate that Babbleskin experience the war first-hand, but the gray-haired ruler had long past his prime, and he'd only be used as an observer. I can still so vividly remember his large silhouette valiantly watching over Garden Valley. Physically, he had little more to give, but his mere presence helped lift our spirits. His legacy was now in our hands.

Rabbitskin and Rilo rode to my side with Harry and Milra close behind.

"I see you've found a new friend," Rabbitskin said, looking over the Quizerant. "He seems awfully ornery. You two chaps have a lot in common."

"Careful," I warned. "Pattyon looks frightfully hungry."

"Indeed," the apeman replied.

I turned to Harry. This wasn't gonna be easy for him. Somewhere deep inside, he probably felt like a turncoat. Regardless, there we sat, father and son, together, the way it should be.

Fellskin and Yora pulled beside Rabbitskin, Bowskin and Tanjo moved to the far side of Harry. My team was in place.

The Three stood on the cleared path before us. Ben and Mr. Malone still looked disoriented, but not my mother. She didn't flinch. She locked her frigid eyes on Harry. Mommy was pissed.

"Soooo, Harry," she said, in a sinister voice I didn't recognize. "I see you've let our son and these Neanderthals trick your mind. Do you really think this ragtag army is our equal? If you wish to save these peasants, hand over the Carnavorines' secrets. Then we'll go far away and leave you here to rot."

"For far too long we've blamed the apemen for our weaknesses," Harry shouted. "No more! I'll no longer stand with you. And we won't allow your treachery to pollute this universe any longer. If you won't abide by reason, you'll perish."

Now, I'd seen this sort of standoff before in movies, babbling back and forth until your enemy gets the jump on you. I could see it starting to play out. Time for talking was over.

"Fhey fhor fhik," I yelled.

Keeya leaped from my shoulder, clamped down on my mother's head, and ripped it from her body. Pattyon was close behind. The Quizerant tore through Ben and Mr. Malone like hot butter.

The battle had begun.

The Three's mangled bodies disappeared. Where they'd pop up next was anyone's guess.

"Move!" I screamed. "Spread out!"

Within seconds, I heard a sickening sound coming from the valley of animals. One of the Godlings had obviously met another gruesome end. Minutes later, a similar grisly noise came from the direction of the Protectors. The war was in full swing.

This grim game of Cat and Mouse continued for hours with complete success. Every time The Three reappeared, they were instantly ripped to shreds.

At breathtaking speeds, Pattyon carried me up and down the cleared path as I continually flanked my army to suit the ever-changing conditions. Faster than any creature on the field of play, even the swift sprinting jarts were no match for Pattyon's speed. He leaped over and darted around the other animals at will.

The war raged on without incident for a great long while. With every Godling death, I grew more confident. At that point, each member of The Three must've suffered at least two or three hundred deaths. Everything was going as planned, nevertheless, our luck was about to change.

Somehow Mr. Malone had reappeared in an unoccupied spot of the travel lane. Harry and I saw him at the same time and sped his way. Naturally, the Quizerant reached him first, but not before he'd gained enough power to fire off a damaging blow. Hundreds of boulders from the Canyon Wall were being hurled our way.

"Harry!" I shouted. "Help if you can!"

"I'm on it!" he yelled.

Slapping his hands together, Harry stopped the mountain wall from crumbling any further, but he could do little about the airborne stones. They were already upon us.

The first wave of jumbo rocks began to pelt down upon the battlefield. Any unfortunate soul in their path was flattened. Many Protectors and creatures would die before this merciless barrage was over.

As the enormous stones fell, Rabbitskin noticed his King sitting helplessly on the hillside and rushed to help. This turned out to be a near-fatal move.

With his back to the Canyon Wall, Rabbitskin couldn't see the last boulder heading straight for his head, but Babbleskin could. The King kicked Yollow in the side and charged. At full speed, they slammed into Rabbitskin and Rilo, narrowly knocking them out of the path of the oncoming rock. The sizable stone buried the King and his Protector where they stood. They never had a chance. Babbleskin had given his life to save my best friend, and for that, he'll always have a special place in my heart.

There was no time to mourn the King. The lethal hailstorm had left many holes in our armor, and The Three wouldn't stop coming. We'd just witnessed, first-hand, the severe consequences of one tiny slip up.

Rabbitskin stared in disbelief at the house-sized boulder that entombed his beloved King. A lone tear ran down his hairy cheek.

"Mount up!" I shouted, trying to deflect his focus. "There's no time for this now!"

Rabbitskin jumped on Rilo and rode to my side. We looked over the war zone and tried to come to grips with the severe damage inflicted by the shelling. Like giant tombstones, massive rocks were strewn across the entire valley. The Canyon stones had caused widespread devastation. The casualties were immense.

Regrettably, the poor souls from the Black Willow Swamp had suffered most. The sightless creatures were sitting ducks during the onslaught. Maybe I'd made a big mistake summoning them to Garden Valley. As their fatalities mounted, I began to second-guess my decision. Since the battle had begun, they'd been taking it squarely on the chin.

To my delight, the falling rocks hadn't slowed my Animal Army. Instead of being demoralized, the survivors were now mad as hell and working together stronger than before.

Springlegs, slyths, and jackal bears had now intermingled with the Protectors. There was no more cleared path or assigned positions. The campaign had become a fast-moving free-for-all.

Thousands of varicolored birds blanketed the sky, screaming instructions to the slugfest below. Their keen vision was essential for helping the animals comprehend where The Three might pop up next. They acted as a perfect radar system.

Suddenly, an irritating, squeaky voice pierced through the noisy battlefield.

"Yoo hoo Ohhh, Logan!"

This can't be good, I thought.

I reluctantly turned around to see my mother standing on top of the largest boulder in the center of the field. It was just bad luck she happened to materialize there. She had both hands stretched high in the air, only inches apart. If her fingers touched, and she had enough time, it was over. Her cynical grin was more than I could bear. She thought she'd won. So had I.

"Young Mr. Spencer," Rabbitskin yelled. "Have you forgotten about your old college mate, sir? Mr. Jack Gerds."

Damn, I thought. Rabbitskin was right. Somehow, during the ebbs and flows of the battle, I'd completely forgotten about the Oh-Philly-Oh Tube.

The last thing my mother saw was me and Pattyon vanish in the distance. Before she could clasp her hands together, both arms were sliced off by the Quizerant's deadly claws. Her blood-stained body went limp and crumpled down between her dismembered limbs.

As she dissolved away, I hopped off Pattyon to inspect the boulder we'd landed on.

"This may be just what the doctor ordered," I said out loud.

Chapter 37

Mr. Malone's canyon shower had provided me a tailor-made lookout station. This Watch Tower was ideal. If I needed to use the Oh-Philly-Oh Tube again to achieve pinpoint accuracy, I'd have to see my target unobstructed. Trust me, it isn't easy calculating the molecular content of structural atoms using Triversic Physics at the power of nth. My mother had sealed her fate giving me a clear line of sight; well, that, coupled with her big fat mouth.

For several hours I closely monitored the fight below. Having a bird's-eye view not only helped me oversee the troops, but also revealed many pleasant surprises.

Sure, the Protectors, slyths, and larger animals were a formidable ground force, but the pint-sized critters were also taking it to The Three — Hard! These smaller creatures were playing a huge role in the struggle. The first fatality I witnessed showed me the devotion of each and every varmint in the valley, and that size, really doesn't matter.

Ben popped up beneath my location in another dangerously vacant area. I was about to act when I noticed a funny-looking rodent about 50 feet from him. It was a pigtail porcupine, a cuddly fuzzball at first sight, but with one deadly feature. This overgrown rat could shoot poisonous quills a hundred yards with remarkable accuracy. The stabbing darts hit Ben like rapid gunfire, each carrying the venom of 30 black mambas. He dropped like a anchor. Lucky for us, these hellcats were strategically positioned all throughout the war zone. Miniature lethal arrows were flying around like heat-seeking missiles.

Nothing was having a greater impact than the acid bees from the Cliffs of Conundrum. They were well-organized, fast, and worked in packs like wolves. What made them so menacing, however, was their toxic sting. Once their stingers hit, the injected Boranium Acid would melt the Godlings into liquid goo. The foul-smelling toxin was so concentrated, the process was over in mere seconds. After watching this demonstrated several times, I was awfully glad the persistent boogers were on our side.

The most clever critter on the battlefield that day was the swirly tail mongoose. These suckers had 70-foot-long tails with 50,000 volts running through them. They'd all banded together and were using their talents in the most ingenious fashion. They didn't go to the fight, they let the fight come to them.

Every swirly tail mongoose had gathered on the west side of the valley. This was now an off-limit grid where other animals dared not venture. They positioned themselves about 50 yards apart and pointed their blazing tails straight up in the air. From my vantage point, they looked like bright red power poles that covered many acres, probably, one tenth of the battlegrounds. A death-dealing high-voltage fence was created.

Flashing lightning bolts flickered back and forth between the mongooses' tails. This punishing power grid would turn anything within its matrix into instant burnt toast. Periodically, one of The Three would manifest inside this unforgiving network. When they did, it was all over but the crying. The swirly tail mongooses were responsible for more kills than any other creature, all without moving a muscle.

The skunk-head dung beetles from Brown Grass Plains were literately dropping bombs everywhere. These 20-pound bugs followed the dinosaur migration year-round, filling their bellies. After gobbling down piles of feces, their gut-churning meal would fester inside them for weeks. When it was time to expel, their highly flammable methane patties would explode on impact. The beetles could dump at will and hit a moving target from a mile in the sky. All across the valley, their stinky mortar shells were blowing The Three to smithereens.

I could go on forever about the amazing creatures I saw that day, sitting atop the Watch Tower. There's just not enough time. There were so many unsung heroes.

Okay, just one more. This one's too good to pass up.

The potbelly blood bat was the only creature on Rabistca that called both the Black Willow Swamp and the Jimini Jungle home. In the long history of the planet, only one living thing had evolved to coexist in these two contrasting environments.

The curious-looking mammal had the traditional wings of a bat, the body of a pregnant hippo, and an enormous proboscis, the syringe-like blood sucker on a mosquito. To give it some scale, it was the size of a water buffalo with a 20-foot wingspan.

The strange recluse lived a simple life, hanging upside-down, high up in some dark, dreary tree inside the Black Willow Swamp. Dangling from his hidden roost, the bat would hibernate for a year at a time, never moving, not even a twitch, until it was time to feed.

The swamp provided a perfect environment for the bat's sleeping requirements, but not as a food source. The creatures there were mostly cold-blooded entities with tough, scaly skin, much too hard to penetrate. To sustain its life for another year, it would need lots of blood, and next door, blood was plentiful.

Once a year the potbelly blood bat flew to the Jimini Jungle to seek his annual victim, and we're not talking peewees. Elephants were his drug of choice, or anything bigger.

Once his Proboscis was dug into its host, the thirsty bat could drain the sufferer dry in less than a minute. Afterwards, with his belly fat and overflowing, he'd clumsily fly back to the swamp where he'd sleep again. His metabolism was that of a large anaconda.

There was only one potbelly blood bat in Garden Valley that day, the only one in the proper rotation cycle. The few others were too full or sleepy to make such a long flight.

Since the start of the campaign, the bulky mammal had been hovering over the battlefield with little success. I first noticed him perched high upon the rim of another fallen boulder.

Every now and then, the leisurely bat would plunge down over the valley, hoping for mere lucky timing. Over and over he tried, but to no avail. After each unsuccessful pass, he'd return to his rocky overhang to rest.

Eventually, his tireless efforts paid off.

In the course of one of his many sweeps, my mother happened to materialize directly in his path. The dark angel jabbed his bloodsucker into her stomach at full speed. With one mighty slurp, he emptied her fluids until she was nothing more than a flimsy sack of skin. Even her eyeballs were sucked from their sockets into the beast's stomach.

The victorious bat flew to the Watch Tower and proudly flicked the deflated carcass into the air. As it floated downward, it slowly dissipated. It was only one death, but a symbolic one indeed. The Black Willow Swamp was officially in the game. They had, at last, registered their first kill.

The potbelly blood bat was tired. It was in his DNA to sleep after each feeding. The blood he milked from my mother would be just enough fuel to power his trip back to the swamp. Soon he'd need a much larger meal to sustain his hibernation, but he'd have to wait until the planetary truce was lifted.

I called out to the big fellow, telling him to return home.

My message was simple. "Job well done."

Chapter 38

I stood on the Watch Tower for a long time studying the warfare below. At some point, I realized the conditions on the ground were rapidly changing. With each new kill, The Three's reoccurrence rate was somehow speeding up, causing the gap between manifestations to become shorter.

Although my animal army was growing weary, they needed to stay crisp. This new accelerated pace only increased the odds of someone slipping through the cracks.

The blistering war zone had become so treacherous everyone was now struggling with the developing fast-paced tempo. Harry, much slower than the Carnavorines, had already suffered three or four deaths by simply not being able to get out of the way. I was unaware of this until I spotted him stumbling around adrift without his Protector, who, sadly, was most likely dead.

Naturally, once I realized the severity of the situation, I used the Oh-Philly-Oh Tube to transport my father to the security of the Watch Tower.

"It's getting ugly down there," Harry said, trying to catch his breath. "The Carnavorines will be next to fall. And when it happens, they won't be as fortunate as me. GO!"

Within minutes, I had all three Carnavorines and their Protectors safely upon the Watch Tower, and from the looks of it, I'd recovered them just in time. The apemen were beaten, battered, and bruised.

Yora and Tanjo began licking each other's wounds. Both were covered head to tail with cuts, scrapes, and dried blood.

Rabbitskin jumped off Rilo and rushed to the edge of the boulder. "What in bloody hell is going on down there, sir?"

I walked over and stared down at the valley. The once-green grasslands had been trampled and stomped into a sloppy mud pit. The Rainbow Roses had been pummeled to mulch. There wasn't a single stalk standing. I searched for the playful butterflies that once so delightfully inhabited this sacred place. There were none. It was almost too much to take.

"Who the hell is that?" Harry yelled.

"Where?" I said, looking around.

"Over there, by the woods. Is that a Carnavorine?"

Right away, I began to recall something Rabbitskin had told me on our way to Rabistca — when one dies, another is born. Only hours after birth, we become full grown adults who instantly possess the full knowledge and knowhow of our ancestors.

It was the only logical explanation. The lost Carnavorine was Babbleskin's replacement.

"Well, I'll be damned," I muttered.

Of course, Rabbitskin had already figured this out.

"If you would, good sir," the apeman politely requested. "Go and retrieve that young chap. He might be a tad bit discombobulated. Wouldn't you say?"

I couldn't contain myself and burst out laughing. Between the poor greenhorn's bad timing, and Rabbitskin's new three-dollar word, I lost it. One by one, my Inner Circle began to crack-up until we were all rolling in the aisles, and for a moment, the world was good again.

"What name will you give him?" Fellskin asked Rabbitskin, when the laughter died down.

"Preposterous!" Rabbitskin said. "Only the King holds that right."

"You are the King." Fellskin proclaimed. "This is your duty now, old friend."

Fellskin did have a point. Rabbitskin was Babbleskin's rightful heir. Normally, Carnavorine kings would hand over their throne in a lavish, traditional ceremony, but these weren't normal times. Babbleskin was the first Carnavorine ever killed in battle.

I knew what to do. It was time for the apemen's first battlefield commission.

"Rabbitskin is now the Carnavorine King," I simply stated. I bowed. The two Carnavorines bowed. Harry bowed, and it was done.

"Well?" I said to the new King.

"Well what, sir?"

"Well, what's going to be the newbie's name? We're all waiting."

Rabbitskin pulled on his chin hairs, crunched his eyes together, and made a smothered gurgling sound deep inside his throat. "Hmmmm, let me see."

This ought to be good. I thought.

"Ah ha," Rabbitskin finally said. "The young chap shall be known as Warskin. He'll be assigned to the Forest section of Rabistca and be an Observer."

"Perfect," I said.

"Very appropriate." Harry agreed.

The new king had performed his first official duty, but there was no time to celebrate. The conflict was still raging beneath us, and it was getting faster and more unpredictable by the minute.

I traveled through the Oh-Philly-Oh Tube to retrieve Warskin. He was still stumbling around, lost at the border of the Universal Forest. I materialized farther down the tree line so he could see me coming. He was probably freaked out enough without me just grabbing him out of thin air.

As I was running toward him, I heard an awful commotion inside the woods. There was a big crunching pop, followed by Ben's mangled body being heaved from the forest. Like a bullet, his corpse burst through the tall trees sailing high over my head.

I eased over to the woods' edge.

I couldn't see anything on the forest floor, but I could hear strange chattering sounds and the loud rustling of branch and limb. I didn't investigate further. Better not push my luck. I'd left Pattyon back at the Watch Tower.

I hurried over to Warskin, seized him by the arm, and we disappeared. When I reappeared, the newborn Carnavorine was no longer with me.

"Where's Warskin?" Harry asked.

"Dropped him off at Sina. This is no place for a novice."

"Good thinking," Rabbitskin said. "He'll be better off there."

"There's something in the woods," I said, pointing to the trees. "I can't figure it out."

"That's our perimeter defense," Bowskin proudly said.

183

"The punch monkeys," Fellskin added. "And I must say, they're doing a wonderful job."

After we'd left for the Halls of Goya, the punch monkeys began arriving at Garden Valley in droves. These normally docile fruit eaters inhabited the Jimini Jungle in great numbers, living a peaceful life in the tops of the tallest trees. Residing so high up, for the most part, kept them out of danger and allowed them to breed and multiply like rabbits. The few predators dumb enough to try and snag one for a presumably easy meal were in for a rude awakening.

The punch monkeys were tiny, only about 2-feet tall. Their hands, however, were humungous. The odd-shaped rascals could make a fist the size of a bowling ball. Through evolution, their hands had gradually increased to enormous sizes. Clutching the massive, thorny limbs of the jungle required extremely large hands, uncommonly strong forearms, and a powerful grip.

Creatures in their habitat learned real fast not to piss them off. With one good uppercut, a punch monkey could send a predator sailing 500 yards on the fly. They packed one hell of a punch.

Fellskin and Bowskin came up with a wonderful idea on how to use their expertise.

It only stood to reason that occasionally The Three would stray off course and manifest inside the forest surrounding Garden Valley. This could cause big problems. The large trees and dense foliage could hide them long enough to do serious damage. The apemen saw this as a potential nightmare, but they also saw an opportunity. Trees were the monkeys' natural habitat. They could swing through the canopies with lightning speed, and there were thousands of them available.

The mini primates would be stomped to death in the open field, so the two Carnavorines stationed them inside the woods surrounding the entire valley. In every tree and on every limb, they sat, patiently waiting for a one-sided game of fisticuffs. When the inevitable happened, the monkeys would descend from their branch, rear back, and knock their target back to the garden.

Looking back, without the punch monkeys, we didn't stand a chance.

Fellskin and Bowskin's foresight had saved us, at least temporarily. We had a new problem. Throughout Garden Valley, the ground began to shake, rumble, and split apart.

Something or someone was causing an earthquake.

Chapter 39

"It's The Three!" Harry yelled. "They're learning."

"Learning what?" Rabbitskin screamed.

There was no time to respond. The Watch Tower began to unmercifully jerk up and down and violently shimmy side to side. The dreadful sound of crunching rock made it almost impossible to hear, and everyone was struggling on the wobbly stone.

The Carnavorines had fallen to their knees and were holding on for dear life. The Protectors were all bouncing around like rubber balls. No one was safe.

The only exception was Pattyon. The Quizerant's sharpened, hooked nails had no problem penetrating the steely stone. He dug in deep and was riding the shock waves like a champion surfer. Even in the most sufferable situations, Pattyon carried a certain coolness.

One thing was for sure; if we were having this much trouble with our footing, so was the Animal Army. Something had to be done.

"I know what it is!" Harry shouted, jiggling and wiggling beside me.

"What?" I shouted back, getting tossed onto my side.

"IT'S THE DEAD ZONE."

Of course, I thought. The Three had somehow figured out a way to use their powers inside the Dead Zone, that five seconds to five minutes it took to re-form after each kill.

We knew The Three's reoccurrence rate had been speeding up as the battle progressed. This had to be why. They were actually trying to get back to the Dead Zone.

"Harry!" I cried out. "You know what we have to do?"

"I do," he screamed. "And we must do it now!"

"What's going on?" Rabbitskin yelled, crawling up to me on his stomach.

"There's no time to explain," I shouted. "Call Keeya, have her spread the word. Harry and I are to be put on the Hit List. Until further notice, we're to be killed alongside The Three. Make sure she tells the Animal Army no exceptions!"

"But why, sir?" Rabbitskin pleaded.

"JUST DO IT!" I insisted.

"Sho Shik Shor Shey Shi Shi Seit," I called to Pattyon.

The Quizerant didn't hesitate. He ran over to Harry and chopped his head clean off. Before his severed head touched the ground, Pattyon had turned his wrath on me. The last thing I remembered was looking up at my headless body, then the lights went out. I had entered the Dead Zone.

The Dead Zone was a fourth dimension of pain, loneliness, and chaos unimaginable. The first time I experienced it, I was on the verge of insanity. I was even happy to manifest again, just to be torn apart by a water wolf. Being eaten alive wasn't fun, but at least I wasn't in the Dead Zone. Void of color, emotions, hope, happiness, or light, nothing could exist in this dark region except total nothingness.

After two or three painful deaths, I was wondering if I'd made a mistake. How could I find The Three in this wretched place? Why had I come to these unholy grounds?

As I was losing all hope, cutting through the despair came the sweetest sound I'd ever heard.

Logan? Logan? Son, can you hear me. Logan?

It was my Maze-O. It was working. We couldn't talk in the Dead Zone, but we could think.

Suddenly, I re-formed and was thrust back upon the battlefield. Damn it! I thought. I was so close to making contact. Fortunately, a monster left hook from a punch monkey knocked me back into a direct line of communication with my father.

Harry! I can hear you. But I'm lost. Help me.

Logan, I've found the source of the problem. Harry communicated. *In the fourth claticlose above the ninth fennored, there's a tiny tear in the outer crust of the Dead Zone. The Three are using it to wreak havoc. If we don't plug it soon, Rabistca will be ripped to shreds."*

How can I find it? I messaged.

You can do it. Harry messaged back. *But you must calculate in reverse. Everything is backwards in the world of the dead.*

I wiped my mind completely clean, focused on the darkness, and let the blackness take me. As I traveled deep into the hidden despair, I began to unravel the secrets of the lifeless kingdom.

It had taken The Three hundreds of deaths to learn how to manipulate the dark world; for me, a mere dozen kills. Harry, who'd been to the Dead Zone many times in the past, had an easier time adjusting.

When I finally found the fourth claticlose above the ninth fennored, it was almost too late. The earthquake had taken a heavy toll on my Animal Army, leaving a devastating path of destruction in its wake.

As Garden Valley shook harder and harder, the creatures on the ground scrambled to stay effective. Many plunged head-first down deep craters. Others were swallowed whole by mother Rabistca, never to be seen again.

The large trees of the Universal Forest began to uproot and tumble over, sending numerous punch monkeys to their graves. The frightened little monkeys were letting out horrific screams as they scampered about trying to avoid the deadly projectiles being tossed around the fragmented forest.

We were beginning to lose the war. We needed a miracle. And a miracle came.

As the ground animals became virtually useless, the eagles, cacks, digtails, hare-clippers, and swoop-claws descended down from the heavens. The birds weren't affected by The Three's devious plan. They weren't bound by soil, root, or stone.

Ancient winged lizards joined the hunt, sweeping through the valley with phenomenal precision and unforgiving results. Believe it or not, three species of airborne reptiles remained on Rabistca. Two had decent numbers.

There were the Rhamphorhynchus and Dimorphodon from the Jurassic period, and the Quetzalcoatlus from the late Cretaceous period.

The Dimorphodon were the smallest and quickest. They had a 4-foot wingspan, a huge head with deep, wide, toothed jaws, and a diamond flap of skin on the end of a long, pointed tail.

The Rhamphorhynchus was a bit larger, with a 6-foot wingspan. They had a long, narrow jaws with sharp teeth that pointed outward. With one good bite, they could turn the Godlings into Swiss cheese.

The most successful creature in the newfangled aerial campaign were the 12 remaining Quetzalcoatlus in existence.

Quetzalcoatlus was the largest flying animal ever created by the Carnavorines. Its enormous wingspan was just under 36-feet wide, with a 10-foot-long neck, big narrow head, 7-foot legs, and a toothless long, thin beak. It was the crown jewel of the legendary Carnavorine creator, Bigskin.

Millions of years ago, Bigskin created dozens of flying creatures that still grace the heavens of a thousand planets. Although hailed by the Carnavorines of his day, he just never seemed happy. As a birdologist, Bigskin was limited in his abilities to create what he loved most, bigness. He always had this thing about the biggest creatures. The apeman was enamored by them.

Always the perfectionist, trying to outdo himself became Bigskin's lifetime obsession. Happily, toward the end of his life, his persistence finally paid off. As a labor of love, he created the Quetzalcoatlus.

One day while traveling through Hillside Hollow near Mt. Skylar, it hit him. Hollow! That's how he'd do it.

Bigskin spent the next 200 years locked inside the Green Houses buried in his work. There, he incubated and delivered his life-long dream. The Quetzalcoatlus was lightly built with hollow bones. Despite being extremely big, they weighed less than 300 pounds.

The 12 Quetzalcoatlus crisscrossed the valley, scouring the area searching for the enemy. They flew in disciplined patterns, which allowed them to carpet the battlefield. When they went in for the kill, justice was swift.

Between the prehistoric flying lizards and the rest of the deadly birds, The Three's strategy was backfiring. Having said that, all the news wasn't good. The tear in the Dead Zone was getting bigger; if we couldn't seal it soon, we were finished.

With each new death, Harry and I found it easier to reach the region of the Dead Zone where the harmful rip was located. We were mindful, however, not to make our presence known. The element of surprise had worked before and would probably serve us well again. Although it was critical to stop the devastation, we had to be patient. One more oversight and we'd all be pushing up daisies.

My father and I began to communicate as only he and I could. Whether we were inside the Dead Zone, the real world, opposing realms, manifesting, or being killed, we could now stay in constant contact.

Planning the battle, I thought I'd covered all the angles. Regrettably, I'd overlooked the Dead Zone, a place where our enemy had been left unwatched and unattended; an intolerable misread.

While inside, The Three learned how to find each other, join hands, and chip away at the darkness. After a tireless campaign, they finally broke through. A microscopic laceration appeared.

Utilizing this tiny pinhole, the Godlings could unleash enough combined power to shake Garden Valley to its foundation. As the hole got bigger, so did the earthquake. It was now a full-blown 8.7 on the Richter Scale and getting stronger by the minute.

I was beginning to lose hope when Harry informed me, using his Maze-O — *I can stop this.*

How? I answered.

Return to the Watch Tower and take yourself off the hit list, Harry instructed. *The Carnavorines will need you soon.*

Good, I responded. *Should I remove you from the list, too?*

It doesn't matter, he replied.

What does that mean? I messaged.

I can plug the hole using my body, Harry explained. *But The Three's rampage will then be aimed at me.*

So. I answered. *They should be near the end of their available deaths. You have hundreds more in your pocket.*

You're smarter than that, Logan. What will happen if I receive a death while in the Dead Zone with The Three's hands joined together? Use the Power of Zero to calculate this scenario. Remember to go in reverse.

As usual, Harry was right. If he received a death while already dead, with The Three's hands locked together, the impact would be -1111.333333 diminished to the power of 3333.111111 multiplied by 478,723.145 metric tons of heat, light, and magnetism. In one death-dealing blow, 1,111 would be obtained.

Panic-stricken, I searched every angle of math and science, desperately seeking another solution. I counted and recounted in a frantic process of elimination, hungry to find an alternate, eleventh hour magic bullet.

In the end, all I could communicate was a few frayed words.

Please, Father?

Son, I have a plan that'll end this war. Get back to the Watch Tower and, when the lights go out, stay put. We'll meet again when the Circle runs its course. Don't say anything, just go! GO NOW!

Reluctantly, using my Maze-O, I told Rabbitskin to have Keeya take me off the Hit List.

Whatever you're gonna do, Rabbitskin pressed, *do it now, young lad.*

Then hurry, was my last transmission.

When I reappeared back on the battlefield, I used the Oh-Philly-Oh Tube to transport myself back to the crumbling Watch Tower.

The very second I arrived, there was a tremendous explosion — and the lights went out.

Chapter 40

Following the massive detonation and subsequent blackout, I heard the most dreadful sounds imaginable. There was chewing, chomping, electrical zaps, moans, screams, bones snapping, skulls crunching; morbid upheaval blared from the darkened field below and an unwholesome stench filled the night air.

I was glad I was high on the Watch Tower, as far from the evil ruckus as possible. Thankfully, it didn't last long.

With no forewarning, in a hush, it all stopped.

"What did you do, Harry?" I said out loud, cutting through the soundlessness.

"Is that you, young Mr. Spencer?"

"Rabbitskin?"

"I'm here, too!" Fellskin called out.

"So am I," Bowskin whispered.

"Everyone pipe down," I said. "Let me think."

In the pitch dark, I sat on that cold rock searching for answers, and for a long time, I was stumped. In the end, it was something Harry had said that helped me solve the riddle.

When the lights go out, stay put, he had messaged, which means he knew the lights would go out.

I suddenly realized what happened.

When I was safely out of the Dead Zone, Harry blocked the hole with his body and waited for The Three to take the bait. He was setting a trap. He wanted them to blast him. Harry knew if he positioned himself properly, the energy from the blast would weld the hole shut; problem one solved.

Right before his fatal blow, using the tear in the Dead Zone, Harry shot a death ray at the planet's only source of light. He'd purposely destroyed the Supar.

With the planet darkened, the creatures from the Black Willow Swamp took over. Now in their element, and with The Three totally blind, they made instant mincemeat of their prey. The Godlings were already close to their fatal number, and it didn't take long for the eyeless mutants to mop up.

3,333 deaths had been reached. The Three were dead.

I knew I needed to act. Many animals lay injured, desperate and alone in the dark. For the first time in a while, I didn't know what to do.

"Help me, father," I whispered into the night.

A slight breeze brushed across my face. Something in the outlying wind seemed to be guiding me.

"Harry?" I mumbled. "Is that you?"

All at once, I started getting hot. A fire began boiling inside me that I couldn't control. It felt like hot lava was pumping through my veins.

Without warning, I launched myself high into the air. I reared my arms back and forcefully slammed my hands together. A huge bolt of lightning blasted from my clinched fist, splitting the darkness, and shooting into the midnight sky. A massive explosion once again rocked the planet, and just like that, light returned to Rabistca. I'd made my first Supar. Harry's powers had been passed to me.

As I floated back down to the tattered stone, I looked up and admired my handiwork. Not bad for a rookie, I told myself, not bad at all.

The Carnavorines scrambled to their feet. They were moving sluggishly from the pounding they endured. It was a miracle they'd even survived.

In the end, it was Pattyon who'd saved them. With his claws firmly dug in, the Quizerant had been a Godsend on the flat, slippery surface, and subsequently, a lifesaver. The Carnavorines each took a leg and held on for dear life. Pattyon also saved Yora. With his massive jaws, he locked onto her skin and held her tight until the earthquake subsided.

Sadly, Yora and Pattyon were the only Protectors remaining on top of the lookout station. During the crisis, Tanjo and Rilo bounced off the huge boulder and plunged to their deaths. The Quizerant did his best to save as many as possible, but even he couldn't salvage them all.

Yora crept to the edge of the Watch Tower and began loudly whimpering, calling for her soul mate. Her deep, throaty howls sent a suffocating song resonating across the ruins of the battlefield. The unhappy tune tugged on the heartstrings of every creature who had witnessed all the senseless casualties. Many creatures had made the ultimate sacrifice, and the heavy price of our victory was becoming painfully evident.

As we looked over the devastation, one by one, our hearts began to break. The scene was horrific.

"Harry?" Rabbitskin asked.

I slowly shook my head. I think he already knew. I tried to hold back my tears, but they came anyway.

Rabbitskin walked over and placed both hands on my shoulders.

"Many were lost today, young lad," he reassured me. "But many more were saved."

The Watch Tower got quiet as we pondered Rabbitskin's words.

We'd mourn the loss of our fallen comrades on another day, for now, order needed to be restored. There were thousands of creatures who required immediate medical care and attention. More than ever, leadership was needed.

"Rabbitskin," I said with renewed vigor. "Have every available Carnavorine rush to Garden Valley. That includes Desert, Ocean, and Forest, by any means necessary."

"A fine plan," he said, nodding.

"Use your Maze-O to contact Snakeskin and get the Council moving. Governance is needed here. Snakeskin can alert Sina on his way. Have him empty the city."

"Bowskin!"

"Yes, sir!"

"Your superb organization skills were priceless on the battlefield today. Now use your talent to care for the wounded. Set up a makeshift hospital beneath the Watch Tower. The Animal Army will help you. Have the punch monkeys gather as many Chipala Daisies as they can find. Use the smaller, agile animals to find strong, straight limbs for splints. Every shape and size will be needed."

I paused and looked into the sky.

"Fellskin!"

"Sir?"

"If there's anybody who knows the magical healing powers of the West River, it's you. I've seen many bucket-mouthed pelicans flying around. Have them fly to the West River and fill their mouths full. We'll need plenty of water for drinking and cleaning wounds. It's time to put your expertise to good use."

"I'm on it," the apeman replied. "But how will we hold the water once it arrives?"

"Have the large clawed creatures, moles, and burrowing animals dig a massive hole at the base of the Watch Tower," I said. "Instruct them to plow deep and wide. When the pit is completed, use it as a retaining pond. Inform the pelicans to make as many trips as possible. Tell them to fly until their wings can no longer carry them. If there's any other creatures with similar skills, put them on water detail alongside the pelicans. The triple-pouched kangaroo is one species that comes to mind."

After giving my instructions to the Carnavorines, I turned and shouted to the valley below, "The planetary truce will be in effect until further notice! We must all pull together to care for the wounded!"

Keeya soared across the skyline repeating my orders. It was time to put my plan into motion. Strangely, the Carnavorines were all still standing in place. No one was moving a muscle. Had I not made myself clear?

"Well," I finally said. "What are you all waiting for?"

The three apemen began to snicker.

"What?" I said, looking confused.

"Forgive us, sir," Rabbitskin said. "But a lift off this bloody boulder would be nice."

Laughing, we all gathered in a small circle and I granted their wish.

The Carnavorines had their orders, but before I could get involved in the cleanup, there was something I had to do. It was time to say goodbye to a friend.

Pattyon had fulfilled his duty and was quickly becoming restless and uneasy. Working with others wasn't his strong suit. He was in the killing business, and the killing was done. It was time for his immediate discharge.

I used the Oh-Philly-Oh Tube to transport us to the beach where we first started our adventure. The reclusive cat wanted no glory nor long-drawn-out goodbyes. He merely wanted to return to his life of solitude inside the Jimini Jungle. It wasn't in the Quizerant's nature to show feelings or love. He was more machine than animal, more muscle than heart.

When we arrived, Pattyon slowly strolled back into the jungle and disappeared. He never even turned around. Soon after he entered the forest, there was a thunderous roar. Maybe it was his way of saying goodbye, but more likely, it was a warning to every creature in ear's range to watch out. The King was back!

I tried to be like Rabbitskin and think of something poetic to say. Our greatest warrior deserved nothing less.

In the end, however, I just said what was on my mind.

"There goes one badass mother fucker."

Chapter 41

When I returned to Garden Valley, it was teeming with life. I shot up to the Watch Tower to get a better view.

The retaining pond was getting bigger by the minute. A slew of rustling root hogs were now plastered to the bottom of the pit and were moving earth like mini excavators. These powerful pigs have a dozen long, pointed ivory tusks protruding from their shoveled jaws. Rarely used as weapons, their tapered tusks were normally used solely as a defense mechanism. When threatened, these tunneling freaks could bury themselves underground in a few seconds. Since their average weight is over 2000 pounds, that's saying something. Not to mention, the daunting task of grubbing through the iron roots of the Jimini Jungle.

As more of the rustling root hogs arrived on the scene, the other animals modestly got out of their way. No animal, large or small, could match their digging skills. The bucket-mouthed pelicans would be returning soon. Thanks to the hungry swine, we'd be ready when they arrived.

Fellskin and Bowskin were in the middle of the action, barking orders and motivating the troops. The two scrappy Carnavorines had become strong, fierce leaders practically overnight.

Rabbitskin had already alerted Snakeskin. Sina had emptied. I pictured hundreds of apemen beating their feet like bicycle clowns, storming down the mountainside heading our way.

"Shir Sha Shuo Sho Sho Shi," I called to the heavens.

Within moments the sky above the Watch Tower was overcrowded with eagles, swoop-claws, digtails, and hawks. I needed their help. It was time for the creatures of the Black Willow Swamp to begin the arduous trip back home. They were useless in the world of light.

As recognition for their brave acts and courageous efforts, I sent a flock of birds to guide them safely home. I ordered this bird brigade to fly overhead sounding a signal of praise during their punishing push back to the dreary marsh. The creatures of the swamp would leave

Garden Valley as heroes. They had earned an unspoken admiration among their peers.

As the abominations slithered away, out of respect, every animal in the valley stopped to express their gratitude. It was a well-deserved salute. The creatures of the Black Willow Swamp slowly slithered down the Perigon Trail and out of sight.

Once I feared them; now I'd miss them. Soon the planetary truce would be lifted, and they'd be feared again.

While my Inner Circle was busy carrying out their orders, I decided to do some spring cleaning. I had no delusions of being able to snap my fingers and return Garden Valley to its original state. My powers were still weak compared to Harry's. Only nature could make the valley truly shine again. Nevertheless, maybe I could help speed the process up a little.

First, I needed to do something about the massive, fallen stones cluttering up Garden Valley. The large rocks were eyesores on the once-beautiful landscape. They needed to go back to Cloud Canyon where they belonged; all except two.

The boulder that buried Babbleskin and Yollow would be left to commemorate their bravery on the battlefield. The beloved King had given his life to save Rabbitskin, and this tombstone would be left as a tribute to his selflessness. Eventually, Garden Valley would bloom again and Babbleskin's spirit could roam free through the grasslands for eternity. I felt confident that's what he would've wanted.

The Watch Tower would also remain. Carved in all four sides of the giant landmark would be the words — *For Those Who Fell.* These four simple words would forever honor those who gave all.

As a beacon of hope, this monument would stand so that future generations could understand the sacrifice made on this historic day. Until the end of days, traveling Carnavorines could pay homage to this famous marker, and remember how the misguided greed of a few destroyed so many.

A third, much smaller stone would be positioned at the entrance of the field of Rainbow Roses, which would one day stand proud again. This headstone wouldn't come from Cloud Canyon, but instead be handcrafted from goya marble and erected at a later date. Two lone names would be etched into the rare crystalline limestone — *Harry and Tanjo*. Neither would've wanted a fuss made about them, but they deserved something special.

In the future, everyone who entered the psychedelic flower garden would carry their names with them. Harry and Tanjo's spirits would dance with the Rainbow Butterflies forever.

As I thought of such things, hundreds of Carnavorines began to pour in from Sina. When they first laid eyes on the battle scene, they were in shock. Rabbitskin met with Snakeskin and the Council to tell them the bad news. It wasn't long before word of the King's passing had circulated through the ranks. There were many tears.

Rabbitskin gave them a moment to collect themselves, but not too long. He was now a hardened war veteran and had learned to bury his emotions. There was work to be done.

Rabbitskin was thrilled when Rainskin arrived on the scene. After a brief embrace, she was ready to get her hands dirty. Most female Carnavorines were expert healers, so Rabbitskin instructed her to report to Bowskin. Soon, her hard work and dedication would earn her second-in-command under the apeman, and she'd personally save hundreds in the following days.

Many Carnavorines were sent to fish in the West River. We'd need plenty of food for the Animal Army and incoming Carnavorines for the next several days. Others gathered firewood, built fires and organized a base camp. Sadly, these were the cushy assignments. The worst undertaking was burying the dead.

Many unlucky animals and Carnavorines were put on death detail. It was a gruesome job. Hours of dragging rotting carcasses and depositing them in large crevices created by the earthquake. This was a daunting task. Remember, some of these creatures weighed tons.

Eventually, it was the red elephants, boxtons, and balaboos that would be the backbone of this operation. No one wanted to use the mass grave system, but with so many dead, we had no choice. I can assure you, however, that every last body was handled with the utmost respect. Once every last casualty of war was accounted for, I'd use my powers to close and seal the cracks forever.

For days, Carnavorines poured into Garden Valley to pitch in.

After days of no sleep, when every cut was bandaged, every bone set, and the creatures were all buried, we had a day of mourning. It was a full 24-hour event. I wanted to make sure we gave every last fallen hero their proper respect.

After the wake, everyone was drained. I told them all to take a few days to sleep and rest. I spent those gloomy days alone on top of the Watch Tower. I was still saddened by the loss of my father. I was hurting much deeper than I was letting on.

After a few days passed, and everyone was feeling better, it was time for the sadness to end.

I mean, come on, we'd just saved the whole damn universe.

It was time for a victory party!

Chapter 42

There were hundreds of Carnavorines scattered throughout the valley. I'd never seen so many in one place. Of course, they weren't all present and accounted for. Some had to remain in their respective sections to watch over things.

Remember, most Carnavorines had never seen the Forest side of the planet. Once the King assigned them to a section, they spent their entire lives there. Only Council members were normally allowed to travel freely through the different environments. Regardless, this was a custom that was about to change. Don't get me wrong, Carnavorine customs and traditions were sacred to me, but as the Creator, I was going to have to pull rank this one time.

To honor the day of the great battle, I declared the first official Carnavorine holiday — National Universal Independence Day. Just joking; way too stuffy for me. I actually decided, for the hell of it, to go with — Apestock.

Sorry, but that's what happens when you give someone with a fucked-up sense of humor too much power. Anyway, most of the Carnavorines thought it was cool. Besides, it added a little pizzazz to their usual prim and proper ways. I bet Harry would've gotten a kick out of it.

To commemorate that day, once a year, all available Carnavorines would descend upon Garden Valley for a night of song, dance, fish, whiskey, and fellowship. Apestock would not only give the hard-working Carnavorines a well-deserved break, but would also provide a time for sharing ideas and stories.

On that day, I also made a vow — no matter what I was doing, in this universe or another, I'd always personally attend this special event.

After my business at the gallows, I'd reside in Sina. I never belonged on Earth anyway. The Other Me showed me where I'd live in the future, but until then, Rabistca would be my home. I loved the Carnavorine planet and couldn't wait to explore every glorious inch.

As the festivities of the first annual Apestock began to wind down, it was time to get back to business. There was still one more stop on this adventure — the Halls of Goya. The new King needed to be officially sworn in, not to mention, we had important things to discuss and some uncomfortable decisions to make.

I called for Keeya one last time. My Animal Army needed to be released back to their home environments. Once the creatures had sufficient time to settle back in, there would be a 24-hour grace period. Only then, would the planetary truce be lifted. Prey would once again become fair game. Things would finally be back to normal inside the animal kingdom.

I called for Bowskin to round up the Protectors and march them back to Sina.

"Give them plenty of rest," I told him. "Wait two weeks before putting them back on assignment. They deserve a long vacation."

It was especially hard for me to say goodbye to Yora. Unlike Pattyon, she had a tender side. Before she left, she calmly placed her head against my chest and softly purred. Bowskin had to practically pry her away from me.

"Don't be sad," I whispered into her ear. "When I return, we'll once again glide across the valley."

I thought about the time Harry and Tanjo had raced alongside us. As Yora pulled away, I became choked up. She'd be sorely missed.

As for Fellskin, he'd be returning with the Council to the Halls of Goya. With Rabbitskin taking Babbleskin's place, there was a vacant seat that needed to be filled. For his unwavering devotion and bravery on the battlefield, Fellskin would be promoted to Council Member. He took the news with his normal, big "Yoo Woo!"

Rainskin was left in charge of the injured who still couldn't travel. She and others assigned to her staff would stay in Garden Valley until every last creature had fully healed. There would be no soldiers left behind.

When Garden Valley had mostly cleared, the Council and I formed a circle, and I transported us all back to the Halls of Goya. There, the fate of Earth would be decided.

Harry's introduction of the Maze-O to you Earthlings hadn't been what nature intended. By the bylaws of the ancient Carnavorines, this gave the apemen the right to shut down the living environment that sustained life on Earth.

The third planet from the sun might have to be cleansed, and by cleansed, I mean, everything dies and the Carnavorines start over from scratch.

Chapter 43

Skillskin's lifelong dream was about to come true. For the first time since its conception, every seat would be filled inside the Grand Council Room of the Halls of Goya.

Once we arrived, the Council members began lighting torches again, but this time was different. Without the need to sneak and hide, every torch could be lit. I'd finally get to see the Halls of Goya the way Skillskin had intended. He'd spent decades on the specifics of torch placements alone.

An unspoken excitement spread through the Council, which seemed to magnify with each newly kindled flame. To my surprise, as they worked, the Council Members began to hum a little tune. As the happy apemen whistled along, the sweet sound echoed throughout every corner of the great hall.

In Earth language, the lyrics would've gone something like this:

Somewhere inside the hollow wind, lies the crying sound of a midnight spent.

Creatures call for their far away love, dreaming of home, and lily-white doves.

Carnavorines watch and make amends, with a touch of heart and a grain of sand.

So, here's a cheer for the one who walks with the plants, and trees, and the lonely hawk.

Be patient, young lad, be true. Be patient, young lad, be true. The day will come when you'll find your way home. Be patient, young lad, be true.

After I'd heard the progression a few times, I began to whistle along myself. I suddenly felt an overwhelming affection I'd never felt before. I was finally home.

Once every light was lit and the last note had slowly faded away, the Carnavorines took their respective positions at the marble table, and I took my seat on the once-fiery throne.

Everyone smiled and took a moment to soak it all in.

The first order of business was to vote on the appointments of Rabbitskin and Fellskin. This unanimously passed with flying colors, and Fishskin swore them in with some high-pitched shrieks.

After that was done, Lambskin stood and made an announcement.

"The Halls of Goya is officially open for business, sir. Carnavorine Creator, Carnavorine King, and all Council members, present and accounted for. Any subject that you choose is up for discussion."

"Hear, hear!" everyone shouted.

Now it was time to get down to business.

There was only one subject on everyone's mind — Earth!

Earth's fate would be a subject of great debate. To be totally honest, since we were breaking new ground, there was no history to draw from. Therefore, to me, there was no right or wrong solution. However, the Carnavorines ancient bylaws were clear. Earth could be cleansed, if the Council deemed fit.

This wasn't cut and dry for the apemen. Before this matter was resolved, there would be many opposing opinions and emotional outbursts. Carnavorines took their ancient laws extremely seriously.

Some members of the Council were on the fence, while others, wouldn't budge. To these Carnavorine purists, there was no gray area. The introduction of the Maze-O didn't let things evolve naturally, so Earth must be cleansed, period!

At that point, Rabbitskin reminded everyone that The Four's scheme wasn't the fault of the Earthlings, and that the Council should think long and hard before making such an irrevocable move.

Of course, it was I, in the end, who came up with a compromise. I had to. With countless meetings over many months, this debate had dragged on far too long. Something had to give.

I told you from the beginning that sometimes people with certain knowledge have to make desperate decisions. Well, this is that time. It was up to me to come up with a compromise. Without a cleansing declaration, the Carnavorines couldn't harm any of their creations; therefore, I had to personally carry out this plan.

The main laboratory at Preotec was manned 24 hours a day, but it would have to be destroyed. Some of the Council Members were adamant that all traces of its history must be wiped out. The main laboratory was where we stored all our important work records.

Are you finally getting this now? I had to blow the damn place up. Hundreds were sacrificed to save billions. Do you understand?

My plan wasn't complicated.

I'd reconfigure and hide a Maze-O inside my head that would eventually destroy all the Maze-Os on Earth. By now, you've probably figured out that I allowed myself to be caught. Before I gave my life, though, I wanted the world to know the truth.

Oh yeah, since I'm about to quit transmitting, there's one small wrinkle I forgot to tell you. When my story is over, while every Maze-O is being rendered useless, your memory of this transmission will be erased. As soon as my tale ends, you'll forget it.

To you, I'll always be a boy genius who turned into a murdering lunatic. Sorry, it had to be that way; Carnavorines' rules. In the future, you must act natural.

Well, I guess that's it.

As we speak, Henry's coming through the door with some new greenhorn guard, Carl. They're here to escort me to the hanging. I'll say no more. But for your listening pleasure, however, I'll leave my Maze-O running so you can hear everything that happens, right up until my neck goes snap!

So long. We'll meet again when the Circle returns ...

"Is this the guy you've been talking about, Henry?"

"That's him, Carl. Let's each take an arm and pull him up."

"So, this is the boy wonder who blew up Preotec, huh?"

"In the flesh."

"Hello, Henry."

"Hello, Mr. Spencer. Are you ready?"

"Yep. And I've got a big surprise waiting for you after my hanging this morning, Henry."

"I'm sure you do, Mr. Spencer. Come along."

"Hey, Henry."

"Yes, Carl?"

"I know I'm new here, but isn't this patient's name Catturd? It says so right here on his chart. Why do you call him Mr. Spencer?"

"Well, son, just to play along with his game, I reckon. You see, Catturd here spent 10 years writing a science-fiction novel and became obsessed with getting it published. Poor guy; no one would give him the time of day. After having so many doors slammed in his face, I guess he finally snapped."

"Is that why he blew up Preotec Publishing and killed all those people, Henry?"

"Probably so, Carl. Every morning when I get him up for breakfast, he says the same thing. Talks about some hanging. He insists you call him Logan Spencer. Logan was a character in his book. I think every night he simply lives out his book inside his head. He's really quite mad. The sad thing is, his novel was pretty good. Hell, I've read it three times."

"What was the name of his book, Henry?"

"Rabbitskin."

The end.